Published by Blushing Books
An Imprint of
ABCD Graphics and Design, Inc.
A Virginia Corporation
977 Seminole Trail #233
Charlottesville, VA 22901

The Alien's Pet
Annabelle Marin

eBook ISBN: 978-1-63954-634-3
Print ISBN: 978-1-63954-635-0

The Alien's Pet

EARTHLY MATES
BOOK TWO

ANNABELLE MARIN

One

Karin Johansson was not a nice woman.

Lawyers seldom were. One of her professors at Harvard Law School had once told the class, "You can either be a nice person or you can be a lawyer. You cannot be both. Nice lawyers don't win cases, and they don't help their clients win."

Karin had taken her words to heart. As a result, at the age of thirty-three, she was a successful divorce attorney at the prestigious Cooper and Mellow, a family law firm. She had risen to the top by following her professor's advice and not being a nice person.

With every case she received, Karin would fight tooth and nail for her client even if her client wasn't a particularly nice person. What Karin cared about most of all was winning. She wasn't above using techniques such as blackmail and extortion, but she wasn't stupid enough to get caught, unlike some of her previous colleagues.

Then there was the money. Yes, the money was nice.

Karin had only been a lawyer for eight years, but she had already managed to purchase a three-bedroom penthouse overlooking Central Park, a luxury car, three highly sought-after designer bags, monthly spa trips, and exactly forty-eight pairs of designer heels. Best of all, she had paid the last of her student loans last year.

To someone who had grown up with money, her purchases might not have been seen as a big deal, but Karin Johansson, one of the most sought-after divorce attorneys, had grown up flat broke.

She and her single mother had lived in a dirty, ugly trailer in Illinois for eighteen years until Karin had managed to secure a scholarship to an out-of-state college. Her useless mother had died a year later, her body finally succumbing to all of the drugs she had been pumping into it since Karin was a toddler.

Karin had spent her childhood and college years eating pieces of stale bread, wearing clothes from thrift stores, and patching holes in her shoes, until she landed her first job out of law school.

Now, she was finally enjoying the fruits of her labor and it was glorious.

So, yes, she might not be a nice person, but she was successful. And to her, it was enough.

Most of the time.

It was eight-thirty in the evening on a Saturday night, but Karin was already freshly showered and dressed in only a comfy robe while sipping a glass of wine. Everyone else her age was probably hitting the newest restaurant or club or getting their children ready for bed.

Meanwhile, Karin was checking her email. She had read the email four times, but she could hardly believe it.

The email was from her bosses, the owners of Cooper and Mellow. It was an email stating they wanted to make her a partner at the firm. The offer letter included a generous salary, a bonus, and a corner office.

Karin sipped her wine. Being made partner before the age of forty, was a dream come true. Yes, her workload would be heavy, but she typically enjoyed the work. Karin would meet more important clientele. Who knew, maybe in a few years she would be able to transfer to another, higher up firm somewhere else. She'd always wanted to live in California.

This was excellent news. Then why wasn't she happy?

Karin was treating the announcement as if she had received a coupon in the mail. She realized for the first time in several years how lonely she felt. Especially, now that she had no one to share the news with.

Karin had never had any friends. People avoided her like the plague when she was in Illinois because she was the poor, trailer trash girl, and Karin was too competitive in college. So much so, it frankly made her unlikeable.

She knew it was lonely at the top. It usually didn't bother her, but sometimes on days like today, it did. Things weren't much better at the office or wherever she went. It seemed everyone around her age was getting married or popping out babies.

While Karin didn't mind following her vow of never getting married or having children, for fear they would meddle in her growing career, days like today made her question things. Would living in the suburbs really be such a terrible fate?

She hadn't dated seriously since her first year of law school, as she found most men dull, irritating, and lacking in conversation. Most men her age either found her too intimidating, came with too much baggage, or were more interested in having her as a Sugar Mommy rather than a wife.

"I have everything I've always dreamed of," she murmured as she served herself another glass of wine. "Then why do I feel like such a loser?"

She made a mental note to only have one more glass of wine and go to bed. Nobody liked a sad, weepy, pathetic mess. Karin decided to finish her wine while overlooking Central Park. There was always something interesting going on, even at night.

The blonde was too busy looking at a pair of dogs chasing each other, she didn't notice something large approaching her penthouse window. By the time she noticed, it was too late.

Something terribly bright was approaching her at top speed.

Then everything went dark.

Two

Karin's head was pounding. At first, she feared she had a bad hangover, which was strange because she only had two glasses of wine. The last time she had gotten drunk had been on the night of her law school graduation.

When the pounding in her head didn't diminish, she had no choice but to wake up. Her heart stopped in her chest when she noticed her surroundings.

The blonde wasn't in her beautifully decorated bedroom. She was in what looked like a dark basement, with very little light.

Worst of all, she was naked. Her large boobs, ass, and even the blonde curls of her mound were exposed in the air as if it were completely normal. Her arms were up, her wrists tied with rope that hung from the ceiling. She felt like a pig who was waiting for its fate at the slaughterhouse.

There were women around her, tied and exposed in the same way. They looked between the ages of eighteen and thirty-five. All of them were different. Some were tall. Others were petite. Small. Curvy. Different ethnicities as well. Most of them were asleep, but some of them were beginning to wake up if the small whimpers were any indication.

This was all a bad dream. It had to be. Nothing made sense.

Karin shouldn't be here. She should be back in her apartment. What was this place?

She looked around again, hoping to find some indication of where she was, but found nothing of worth. It just looked like a creepy basement, which continued to make her uneasy.

The last thing she remembered before she passed out was a bright white light but nothing else. What had happened since then? Was she still even in New York? Had anyone reported her missing?

Her heart sank when she remembered the only ones who would care about her going missing would be her bosses. And only because they would be worried about who would take over her cases. She didn't have any friends or family. Not even a dog would miss her.

What were they planning on doing to her and the other women? Kill them? Torture them? Sell them into prostitution or slavery? No one captured this many women with good intentions at heart.

Karin shook her head. She had to stop thinking. All it was doing was causing her to grow more panicked. She needed to get out of here. She couldn't rescue everyone else, but she could certainly rescue herself.

The ropes which were binding her arms weren't tightly done. She snorted. Her captors probably thought a weak, little woman wouldn't be able to untie herself, which was probably why they hadn't done a very good job, but she was one step ahead of them.

Karin had taken a self-defense class during her freshman year of college. She still remembered everything the dull instructor had told them about how to untie her ropes if she was ever bound.

It took a bit of wiggling, cursing, and using her nails to get the knots undone, but she somehow managed to do it. Karin fell with a loud thud, but she managed to keep her moans to a minimum.

She shivered, her nipples perking up from fear. Karin felt horribly exposed. She had never liked seeing her body in the nude. She had always thought it was too much. Her boobs were heavy, her hips wide, and her butt always made it a hassle to find a decent pair of jeans.

And now, here she was in an unknown location, feeling terribly exposed.

Karin glanced around, looking for some type of weapon. Even a broom would do, but she found nothing. It looked like she would have to rely on her self-defense moves even though her body was feeling terribly weak, as if she had been injected with a tranquilizer.

The blonde forced herself to move to the door, trying her best to ignore the dangling naked bodies. With a trembling hand, she opened the door. The next thing she did was let out a terrifying scream.

In front of her, were three large creatures.

She couldn't call them men because they didn't look like any men she had ever seen. They were tall. Six-five to seven feet tall if she had to guess, with skin that was dark gray and long, pulsing veins adorning the muscles of their chest and arms. Pointy teeth peeked out from their thick lips, and their bulging red eyes were looking straight at Karin.

Karin took a step back. They were monsters. Monsters who would probably eat her for breakfast and use their sharp teeth to pull her apart.

She was screaming herself hoarse. She couldn't remember the last time she had screamed so much. But maybe the screaming would help attract attention.

One of the men, the taller of the three with dark hair,

approached her gently as if she were a frightened cat. "Calm down," he instructed firmly. His voice was firm but not harsh. "My name is Kyvan. You're are going to be all right. No reason to get nervous. You just woke up a little earlier than you should have." He looked at where she had been hanging. "You got out by yourself? Impressive. I forgot how crafty humans are when they are pushed into a corner."

"D-don't come any closer!" she ordered, but her voice was weak at best.

"Enough!" one of the gray monsters with long, red hair barked. "Just put her back to sleep, Kyvan, before she starts making all of the other females nervous."

The man who had introduced himself as Kyvan pulled her wrist before she could even blink. Whoever these monsters were, they were strong and fast. Certainly not human.

What did they mean about putting her back to sleep? Were they going to kill her?

Karin wasn't a woman who cried often, but she found her eyes watering. "Please."

Kyvan, who seemed to be the only one with a conscience of the three standing before her, gave her a sympathetic look. "It won't hurt, sweetheart. I promise. You'll just feel a little pinch. Be a good girl and take your medicine for me." He pulled out a long syringe filled with a blue liquid, which only caused her to panic even more. Kyvan gently placed her over one of his knees so her bare butt was front and center. She was too scared to care about her modesty. She felt a pinch when he injected the needle in her rear end, followed by exhaustion. "Sleep," she heard his voice say. "You'll need it."

When Karin woke up again, she realized she was once again tied. This time, with what felt like metal cuffs. She could only take a guess, though, because she was strapped on her back. She was lying down on a sleek, white table. A flat, floating, rectangular-like object was swishing back and forth from the top of her head to her toes. Karin felt incredibly sore, like she always did when she finished running the yearly marathon the firm hosted.

Her blue eyes looked around the all-gray room. Would it kill these guys to add a little color?

A slightly shorter man than the giants from earlier was looking at the numbers in front of him from a monitor. He looked older and there was an annoyed look on his face. If he noticed Karin had awoken, he didn't said anything.

"Where am I?" she croaked. Her throat felt dry.

"One of the healing rooms. Relax. I am just finishing running a few tests, just making sure everything is where it's supposed to be and everything is working how it should be. The human body is much more complicated than it seems, especially the females. Though, of course, no one listens to poor Azis. The only thing on their mind is breeding—"

"Why does my body hurt?"

"You were given two injections." Azis looked bored. "One to increase fertility, to make sure you get impregnated quickly. The second one is to prolong your lifespan, to make it similar to ours. Humans die so quickly, we want to make sure all of the hassle is worth it. Your private regions have been removed of hair completely. The soreness should diminish in a few days. My supervisors won't like it, but I can give you a pill to remove some of the soreness—"

"What?" Karin screeched. Oh, yes, it was official; her increased stress levels from the past decade had finally made her insane. This man, thing, or whatever just told her they'd prepared her like a prize heifer, to be bred? She started to squirm. "Get me out of here!"

"Subject 206—"

"Karin! My name is Karin! I insist you call me by my name."

Azis curled his lip, obviously in annoyance. He didn't look as scary as the men from earlier, but she didn't want to push too far.

"Karin, I'm afraid it won't be possible. You were handpicked along with every other woman you saw earlier. Taking humans from earth is risky business. We cannot do it often and especially cannot return the females simply because they are upset. You, along with everyone else, were chosen because you were alone. You had nobody who would miss you, which makes things easier." Azis' voice sounded almost kind. Meanwhile, Karin wanted to burst into tears. He was right; she had no one. "You'll see, once you've calmed down, we will find you a mate. You won't be treated cruelly here as long as you obey. Most women settle down after their first baby. Before you know it, you won't even miss Earth."

"What is this place?" The fear had subdued somewhat, but she was sure it was because she was going into shock.

"Krotev. It is an all-male planet. We're not far from Earth, which is why we don't look so different, you and I. Our species has been reproducing with human females for centuries. Technically, I suppose you could call us half-human, though it is not fully correct. When we're born, we are full Krotev aliens, though we change back between a human form and our true form. It is what the warriors do, at least, especially when a woman is particularly nervous."

"All male planet? So, there are no women on Krotev?"

"That's what I just said! Weren't you listening? Our genes makes it so females only give birth to males. Never females. Which means, we have to go down to earth every couple of years or so to get a new batch. Though the king has been going more often. It is a waste, if you ask me, especially with so many other planets close by—"

Karin didn't bother listening to Azis' whining. She would be given to one of these brute men and forced to be his whore and get pregnant over and over again until she gave birth to a boat-load of his demon-looking children.

This would not be her fate. She would make sure of it.

Karin didn't care if it got her killed, she would return to earth if it was the last thing she did.

Three

One month later...

King Korrev looked at his second in command and best friend, Kyvan, with a bored expression. He had just finished his daily training and had been about to enjoy his dinner, when Kyvan asked if he could have a word.

If he would have known the reason behind it, he would have denied his request. Both of them were in their human form, which they preferred to be in when they were not training and, instead, were in the safety of the palace.

The two men couldn't have been more different. While Kyvan sported short, cropped, dark hair, Korrev's own golden blond hair cascaded down his shoulders when he didn't have it braided. Kyvan was even-tempered and fair. Korrev was sharp-tongued and violent.

It was a wonder they were even friends in the first place. But they had grown up together, almost like brothers. For years, they only had each other, as their fathers often fought in wars and their mothers were dead and buried.

As far as friends went, he supposed he could do worse. Besides, Kyvan was the only one who tolerated him when he was in one of his raging tempers which, for the king, was often.

"Are you telling me three Krotev warriors have been struggling to control one single human female for an entire month?" he growled. "Why the hell hasn't she been mated yet?"

Kyvan sighed. "Everyone has refused to take her. They say she isn't worth the trouble and would rather wait for the next batch. She's pretty." As if that solved anything. No one wanted a beautiful female if she had a sharp tongue. "But she's difficult. We have tried everything to break her—placed her in isolation, reduced her food, threatened her, spanked her until her ass was bright red and covered in welts. Nothing works. I think we might have to send her back."

"No. Memory erasing is a hassle."

"Do you suggest we kill her?"

"No. It would be a waste if she's pretty. Bring her to me. I want to see the female who has managed to subdue my strongest warriors."

Kyvan led the king to one of the smallest rooms they usually used for interrogation. One of his warriors, Bazin, who had bright red hair, was guarding the door. He looked embarrassed that they had to get the king's help, as he should have been. How was it they couldn't handle one simple female?

"Kyvan, leave," Korrev instructed. If he was going to break this woman, he was going to do it without him present. He was one of his best warriors, but he was tenderhearted, especially when it came to females. It was best he wasn't here, or it was going to cause problems in the long run.

If he wanted to break this woman and have her understand that she was at the bottom of the totem pole, he didn't need anyone giving her looks of sympathy.

Kyvan looked like he wanted to argue, which he would never do in front of another person. He respected the king too much. He gave a curt nod before he left.

"Bazin, what is the woman's name?"

"Karin, Your Majesty."

"Get a fire going and a hot poker. The ones with my initials and the king's seal." He paused. "And a bow. Pink if we have it. Attach one of the name plates engraved with my initials and the royal symbol."

Every female in Krotev wore a ribbon and bow around her neck. It contained a tracking device.

"Yes, of course."

Once he scurried off, Korrev opened the door. The room was small and cramped. There were no windows, so as to drive their prisoners insane. There was a woman crouched in the corner of the room. Tall. Blonde. Wide curves. Large breasts. If it wasn't for her terrible attitude, she would have been the perfect mating partner.

The woman glared at him with angry blue eyes, as if she wanted to attack him. It wouldn't have been any use, though, even if she tried. He could break every bone in her body without thinking if he wanted to.

Korrev couldn't help but smirk. She was a bit cute, like a snarling animal, as if her small teeth would do anything to hurt him. Perhaps, he should have come in in his true form, instead of the human one, but where would the fun in that be?

Everyone, with the exception of Kyvan, feared him. It was nice to have a challenge for once.

"Turn around," he ordered, waving a finger in her direction.

Karin's jaw clenched, but she didn't move. He waited for a minute. Patience wasn't really his strong suit.

He gripped her arm and jerked her up. "I am King Korrev. When I give you an order, you follow it, understand? My men have been too soft on you."

"Fuck you!" Then the little brat had the audacity to spit on him.

Rage filled his veins, and it took all his willpower not to

strangle her. He pulled her by the ear and led her towards the back of the room where there were two handcuffs hanging on opposite ends.

Karin whimpered as he cuffed both wrists, to prevent her from leaving. Her back was towards him, which gave him a good view of her ass. It was dark pink as Kyvan had mentioned, but it was obvious it was on the road to healing. There wasn't a single welt on it.

He removed his belt, not bothering to bend it in half. "It appears my men weren't hard enough on you. Do not worry, I can easily remedy that so you don't do anything as stupid as you just did."

Korrev landed the belt firmly in the center of her ass. She screamed as he marked her bottom. His belt fell again harshly on the backs of her thighs. Karin whined, but he showed no mercy.

The king whipped her with the belt over and over again, until every inch of her ass from the top to the backs of her thighs was bright red and covered with belt marks. Karin screamed herself hoarse, but unlike his useless warriors, he showed her no mercy.

His cock grew hard as he stared at the plump, round, red cheeks which were practically glowing and bounding lewdly as she shifted from foot to foot, trying to escape his belt. Korrev wasn't usually impressed by the human race, but he had to admit they made beautiful females.

After the fortieth hard stroke on an already tender butt, King Korrev finally stopped. He put on his belt and went towards a sobbing Karin. He pulled on her golden hair to push her sobbing face towards him.

"Listen closely, Karin, because I am not someone who likes to repeat himself. You have given my men enough trouble for an entire month. This misbehavior stops now. You might have been someone on Earth, but you are in Krotev now, and here, you are nothing." He clamped one hand against a swollen cheek and rotated it slowly, his fingers caressing the fresh welts. She sobbed. "I can make your life very uncomfortable." He entered one unlubricated finger inside her tight hole as she flinched, involuntary squeezing his finger inside her tight anal cavity. "So, be a good girl and do as you're told. All right?"

She didn't agree with him, but she didn't argue, either. It was a start.

The door opened and Bazin stepped inside. "Sir, I have the bow and the poker is warm. Where do you want them?"

"On the table," Korrev barked. "And leave. Your services are no longer required."

"Yes, Your Majesty."

Korrev picked up the ribbon with the bow from the table. A name plate with his initials and the royal symbol dangled from it. Much like what a domesticated animal would wear. He placed the bright pink bow around her neck.

Karin's crying had subdued, but she was still trembling.

"Since my men do not find your naughtiness appealing, you will become my pet. Not mate. Pet. You are the lowest of the low, Karin. You are even below the other females. You are nothing." Korrev smiled. "Who knows, maybe with a bit of training, someone will want you as his mate, but until then, you are mine. Do not bother removing the bow. Only I have the key."

"I will never submit," Karin choked out bravely. "Not until I am taken home."

Korrev smiled at her stupidity as he grabbed the hot poker. "That will never happen. Now, I need you to remain still for ten seconds. You are going to feel a burning sensation on your right buttock."

Before Karin could even ask what he meant, he pressed the hot poker in the shape of his initials and the royal symbol into the spanked skin. Karin screamed at the burning sensation as her ass was branded.

"There." The king removed the poker after ten horrid seconds. "You are marked. Everyone will know you're mine."

She didn't seem to be listening. She just continued sobbing. He shook his head. This was not what he wanted to deal with right now. He couldn't stand crying females, which was one of the main reasons why he hadn't taken a mate, even though he should be providing heirs.

Human females were so sensitive. Everything was always the end of the world for them. It was surprising the human species had lasted as long as it had.

"Karin, stop crying!" he ordered immediately.

Karin only cried harder.

Perhaps breaking her wouldn't be difficult after all. He removed the cuffs from her wrists and placed a weeping Karin over his shoulder, her burning, bare rump in the air, and took her back to his quarters.

Karin stopped crying momentarily when he entered his large bedroom. She was the first person to be there other than the servants, and he wondered briefly if it was a mistake. His bedroom was supposed to be his sanctuary. The last thing he needed was a little human running around and ruining his peace.

His bed was large, to accommodate his larger than most frame. One of the servants had placed a small square mattress on the edge of his bed. Pink, to match the bow around her neck.

He dropped her on the bed as gently as he could, but Karin still glared at him. She looked around momentarily, forgetting her anger. "Where am I?"

"My bedroom."

She looked down at her mattress, looking a little lost. "And this is where I'm supposed to sleep?"

"You can sleep on the floor if you prefer." Korrev narrowed his eyes. "Remember, you are a pet. You have no privileges. If I want you to lick the floor, you will lick the floor without complaining, or your ass will pay the price."

She flushed bright red. "My butt hurts," she murmured. Karin winced as her fingers touched the marks left behind. She looked horrified that his initials were on her bottom. On the other hand, it made Korrev feel proud to see her marked with the king's crest.

"I don't see how it is my concern," Korrev answered plainly.

Karin's eyes watered, but she didn't beg. Maybe she did have a little fight left in her. Good. It would be boring for him if she gave up too easily.

"If you need to relieve yourself, you do it in that room." He pointed to a smaller door where she could find the bathroom. "Don't make a mess."

She nodded, looking exhausted. It was still early, but she needed sleep. It had been a long day for her.

Karin settled into her mattress, for once not shielding her nakedness. She needed to get used to being naked. He would never allow her to wear clothes. None of the females in Krotev did.

There was a knock on the door and a servant came in with a bowl of white liquid. He nodded his thanks and delivered the bowl to Karin. "Drink," he ordered.

She wrinkled her nose. He almost smiled. She would make a good queen. Karin was just as stubborn as he was. "What is it?"

"Warm milk."

"This place has milk?"

"We import it along with other human goods and then sell it at the local market. Now, drink." The milk was laced with a tasteless sleeping and healing powder so she would sleep through the night and her bottom would heal. It would still ache in the morning, but not as much as it did right now.

"I need a glass. Or at least a spoon."

"Pets drink from the bowl."

Karin made a face. For a second, Korrev wondered if he might have to force feed her, but much to his surprise, she poked out her pink tongue and started licking the milk from the bowl in his hand.

She was only halfway through when she started feeling sleepy. Korrev pulled the bowl away as Karin settled into her mattress at the foot of his bed and promptly fell asleep.

Korrev watched her sleep for a few minutes before he started stroking her blonde hair, She was quite pretty. They had brought in many beautiful women before, but Karin was quite possibly the most beautiful of them.

The king shook his head. He really must stop thinking the most stupid thoughts.

Four

When Karin awoke the next morning, she was sore all over. Especially on her butt, though it didn't hurt as much as it had last night.

It was strange to still be naked. Even after being in this strange alien planet for weeks, she wasn't used to being nude. Karin had been hoping to be allowed clothes when she had her period, but whatever these monsters had injected her with had made it so she no longer had her menstrual cycle but was still fertile.

Back home, the only time Karin had been naked was when she was taking a shower. Her sex life had been non-existent and even when she'd had one, she hadn't spent hours nude. Now, she was expected to do so and she wouldn't put up a fuss.

Korrev might have shown a hint of kindness, but it was dismal at best. It would be better not to aggravate him too much, unless she wanted her head to be detached from her body. She wondered if someone back home had noticed she was missing yet. Maybe the local news had run some type of report. But she wasn't too hopeful. Lonely woman goes missing? It wasn't much of a headline if she was being completely honest.

She uncurled from her bed, which was surprisingly comfortable, and looked over towards the big bed, expecting the king to still be asleep. He wasn't. The bed was empty and unmade. She wondered where he was.

Before Karin could be thankful for her good fortune, another door opened, exposing Korrev. He was dressed in dark gray clothing and a long red cloak. His blond hair was pulled back in a simple braid. He looked tense and annoyed, even though it was still early.

Karin noticed all of the Krotev warriors wore clothes, but none of the females who had been kidnapped, which seemed terribly unfair. Korrev also seemed to prefer his human form, or maybe he wanted Karin to be spared a heart attack. Whatever the reason, she was grateful she didn't have to see the hideous gray figure skulking around like a demon.

Her stomach grumbled and she blushed. Karin was hungry. She had been protesting most meals during her captivity, but now she would sell her kidneys for a double bacon cheeseburger.

"Good, you're awake." Korrev turned to face her, then before she could even say anything, he walked towards her until he was standing over her like an overbearing mountain.

For a second, Karin worried he was going to spank her again, but instead, he pulled down his pants, exposing his long, thick pink cock. Karin felt herself grow red and she would probably lie down in shock if Korrev hadn't been pressing his hand against the back of her head as his cock rubbed against her face.

"Suck," Korrev commanded.

Karin grew even redder. Did he seriously expect her to suck his cock as if she were a sex slave? Sure, he had labeled her a pet, which wasn't a better nickname, but she hadn't expected to be forced to get on her knees.

"I will not—"

Korrev, being the sadistic asshole he was, used the opportunity to stuff his already erect cock in her mouth. She grimaced as she felt his hot, heavy manhood inside her mouth. Karin felt like she was already at her limit. He wasn't exactly a small man, but he continued to force himself inside her mouth until she had taken every inch.

"Suck," Korrev ordered, tugging on her blonde hair to make sure she wasn't trying to pull away. "This is the second time I asked. If I am forced to ask a third, you will get a welted bottom in addition to sucking me off. I suggest you do as you're told. Especially when I am asking nicely."

Tears of embarrassment pooled at her eyes as Karin felt his warm dick throbbing inside her mouth. This was asking nicely? It was assault. If they were back on Earth, she would hit him with a lawsuit that would force him to spend a nice amount of time in jail, in addition to paying her a large amount for pain and suffering.

But they weren't on Earth. Karin was just a pet. She didn't have power, and Korrev knew it.

He was a bastard, and as soon as Karin was able to, she had plans to burn his dick right off. For now, she just focused on sucking because she didn't want to end up with another sore bottom. Karin didn't even attempt to bite his dick off. Korrev seemed to be in a foul mood already.

She would play nicely. For now.

Karin started sucking his thick member, which felt too big inside her small mouth. She had never sucked someone off. It had never appealed to her. She hoped she was doing an okay job and he wouldn't punish her for her lack of knowledge.

The blonde must have been doing something right because Korrev groaned almost immediately as he ran a hand through her hair and began fucking her mouth. He thrust inside her, back and forth, his length rubbing against her cheeks.

It wasn't unpleasant, Karin finally decided after a while. Even though it was a bit hard to breathe, especially when he forced her to take all of him inside her mouth. His member felt unusual in her mouth. Big, of course, but also warm and slippery.

Karin was just getting used to the sensation when she felt him erupt inside her mouth. Her mouth was suddenly filled with his hot and sticky cum. She grew furious. Would it have killed him to give her a little warning? She did not want this man's seed inside her mouth.

Korrev pulled out and she was ready to throw his cum out, but the bastard shut her jaw closed with his hand. He looked at her with his sharp blue eyes as she kneeled down in front of him. Karin suddenly felt very small and worthless. "Swallow every last drop, Pet. It's what good pets do. They swallow their master's seed."

Karin shut her eyes tightly to avoid looking at him while she was on her knees drinking his load. It didn't taste as bad as Karin had anticipated. It was even a little bit sweet, but it still didn't mean she appreciated being forced to taste it.

He rubbed the back of his hand on her head, making her feel his heavy rings. "Good girl," he murmured, sounding pleased. "You can expect to suck me off every morning before breakfast." She opened her mouth to protest, but he shook his head. "It wasn't a suggestion; it was a command. You either suck me off, or you can expect to get your little ass whipped instead. Your choice."

Hot, angry tears of humiliation threatened to spill out. Even Karin wasn't sure if she could contain them this time. So many humiliating things had happened to her in such a short span. There was only so much humiliation she could take. She was a proud woman and she felt like she had been reduced to a simple object.

Korrev took her silence as submission. He used this thumb to wipe away some of the leftover cum which had dripped from the side of her mouth. He placed his cum-coated thumb inside her mouth. "That's a good pet," he murmured. "You're learning your lesson very well. Who knows, maybe by the end of the year, I can find someone who would be willing to breed you without fearing you will bite his cock off."

I will never submit! she silently screamed as he removed his thumb from her mouth. *Never!*

Korrev patted her bottom, specifically the side where she had been branded. She let out a small squeak. It was still tender, though it wasn't burning like it had yesterday. "Let's eat breakfast."

The king led her to an adjoined room where there were hard-looking chairs and a table set for two. On the table, there was a small pile of food fit for a king. She didn't recognize most of it, as it wasn't human food. Everything looked brightly colored and slimy.

However, she was so hungry that, at this point, Karin would eat dirt. Besides, she had eaten some of their food during captivity and it wasn't too bad. Karin reached for a chair, but her new master pulled her back.

"Pets eat on the floor, beside their master."

Karin narrowed her eyes. "You must be joking."

He raised a pale eyebrow. "Kneel on the floor, or you can starve."

Her grumbling stomach gave her away as she gingerly kneeled down next to the chair where he would be sitting. The blonde's knees were already red from kneeling so much.

Korrev gave her a satisfied smirk as he sat down. She wanted to punch him so she could wipe the smirk off his stupidly hand-some face. Her ass was still too tender and he looked like the type who would beat it bloody.

Korrev broke off a piece from a fluffy-looking orange loaf. He fed it to her and she was so hungry, she swallowed it whole. The food tasted slightly like bread, but nuttier and with a more orange flavor.

The king continued to feed her small pieces of food, as if she wasn't worthy enough to handle utensils, but all Karin was worried about was satisfying her belly. She ate from his hand in silence, trying not to scold herself for giving up her fight against him so easily.

"Are you satisfied?" he asked after a while. Korrev hadn't eaten much. He had fed her most of the food and he preferred to drink from his goblet.

Karin nodded, wondering how he was planning on torturing her next.

It was a bit surprising he hadn't taken her yet. Hopefully, he never did. Karin would prefer to get her butt beaten red than have him take her with his big cock she had barely been able to fit inside her mouth.

"Good. Follow me." He led her back to his bedroom and pulled out a pink leash, which matched her bow, from the drawer. Korrev dragged her by her bow and attached the leash to her collar. "I have a meeting," he said, as if it should have been obvious. "You're coming with me."

She let out a hollow laugh. "You must be joking. I am not walking around like this, with you dragging me around with a leash like I am some kind of animal."

Korrev tsked in disappointment as he squeezed her left breast tightly, his thumb pinching her nipple until it was as hard as a pebble. She whined at his sharp pinches. It hurt, but she couldn't ignore the throbbing which had also appeared between her legs. Damn her traitorous body.

Even when Korrev was punishing her, it seemed he also knew her sensitive spots. "You are a pet. My pet. Where I go, you follow." He slapped her left boob, leaving behind a pink handprint. She whimpered as he tugged on the leash, forcing her to walk outside naked while being led by the leash. "Now come, Pet. You've been a good girl for now. Don't make me punish you."

"Why are you doing this?" Karin demanded. "Isn't it enough

you took me from my home? Do you have to continue to humiliate me by walking me around with a leash like a dog?"

Korrev smiled at her as he cupped her face in his hand. "You humans have a saying I've heard often during my trips to earth. 'Life isn't fair.' This is one of those instances."

The walk through the palace halls was one of Karin's most humiliating moments. Strangely, Korrev's warriors barely blinked in her direction even though she was nude. Some of his warriors lived at the palace, and she saw a couple of women who were equally naked, with bright collars around their neck. They glanced at her curiously, some with pity, but they didn't bother saying hello.

Her cheeks flushed. She really was nobody, like Korrev had mentioned.

Korrev led her to a small room where two elderly aliens were waiting for him. They were in their true form, but since they were older than Korrev, their red eyes and gray skin didn't seem as threatening as when Karin had first seen them.

If they thought Karin's presence was weird or unwanted, they didn't show it. Korrev seemed to be a sadistic bastard. She doubted him leading a woman by a leash was the worst thing they had seen.

"Kneel, Pet." Korrev pointed to the floor next to a shiny gold chair.

Her knees buckled in protest; she was so sore when it came to her lower half, the last thing she wanted to do was kneel, but she did as she was told. Karin didn't want to get spanked in front of these elderly aliens. She could always pick a fight in private where she could at least have some privacy while she was being punished.

Karin had expected the meeting to be short, but after twenty-five minutes of kneeling down while hearing boring conversations about other planets, the only thing she wanted to do was cry. It didn't help that the balls of her feet were constantly touching her sore butt and the area where she had been branded.

When Karin finally felt like she was going to collapse, she had no other choice but to tug on Korrev's bright red cape. "Um, Korrev?"

Korrev gave her a dirty look. "What?"

"My knees hurt," she mumbled. "Can I lie down or—"

Korrev didn't let her finish, he gripped Karin's thin wrist and hauled her up so she was sitting on his lap. She groaned when her welted butt touched his hard knees, but she didn't dare complain. Sitting on his lap was certainly better than being over his lap.

Korrev surprised her by wrapping his arms around her and pressing her against his muscled body while he continued talking about topics which, quite frankly, bored her. Eventually, his hands started to wander.

At first, he just stroked her spanked ass, which she didn't mind because she needed someone to take away the soreness, but then his hands started dipping lower. He parted her legs and started rubbing her bare, pink slit with his fingers.

Karin blushed bright red as she squirmed. Did he have to touch her here in front of everyone? It was so embarrassing.

Korrev pressed a hand on her thigh, to keep her from squirming, his nails from his other hand digging against one of her butt cheeks in warning. Karin's eyes watered with tears, silently begging him not to touch her while his men were staring even if they could care less.

The king's fingers continued stroking her pink cunt until her lower lips swelled with desire even if she was humiliated. Sometimes he would dip one or two fingers inside her as she quickly became wet.

It had been so long since she had been touched by a man, she had forgotten how wonderful it felt, even if he was just dipping his fingers inside her. She didn't want to imagine how it would feel when his heavy cock would split her open.

Karin's cheeks were flushed. She was practically humping his hand as he touched her lazily while he continued to talk politics. His fingers, by this time, were slick with her wetness and she was only growing wetter by the second.

Her thighs were practically trembling, and for once, she forgot all about her red ass. All she could think about was the king's fingers on her cunt.

She let out a series of whines and pleas which sounded pathetic to her own ears. Karin was so close to her release, she could practically taste it, but she couldn't have an orgasm in front of the two alien men. Even if it was quite obvious they did not care, it would be too humiliating for Karin, who had been known as being prim and proper all her life. Maybe a little too much.

"Please," Karin resorted to begging. This was much bigger than her pride. "Please stop. Otherwise, I won't be able to contain myself."

Korrev's strokes between her legs became faster, much to her dismay. When he pinched her engorged clit, she couldn't contain herself any longer. She let out a loud moan which she was sure would be able to be heard through the entire palace as the orgasm spread throughout her body.

She panted while her body shook with the remnants of her pleasure. Karin wanted to deny how good it had felt, but she couldn't. Not even the orgasms she had given to herself late at night could rival this very moment, even if she had been forced to participate in front of onlookers.

Karin had missed having a man touch her body. She hadn't realized how much until today, even if the man was a brutal alien king.

One of the aliens across from her raised an eyebrow, not

impressed by either of them. "Shall we come later, Your Majesty when you are not busy dealing with your pet?"

Karin was still experiencing her post orgasm bliss. She was too tired to be embarrassed.

"Not necessary." Korrev picked her up as if she were a limp doll. "I will put my pet down for a nap, lock her in my bedroom, and then we will continue where we left off." Korrev smirked at Karin, which made her feel uneasy. He brushed his lips against her forehead. "Perhaps it won't be hard to break you after all."

Five

The weeks passed by slowly for Karin, to the point where she quite honestly wished she would be locked in a sort of cell or be forced to live out the rest of her days in an insane asylum, rather than be the king's pet. She despised being the king's pet. Hated it so much.

Karin had had more sex in the last three months than she had in her entire lifetime. Every part of her was sore. Her pussy. Her ass. Her breasts. Even her ass had been attended to by Korrev's punishing fingers.

Every day, it was the same routine. She woke up and was expected to pleasure the king with her mouth. They would then have breakfast, where the king would feed her food. Sometimes she would sit on his lap, while other times she would be kneeling down next to him. Afterwards, Karin would tag along to whatever plans Korrev had for the day. She would be fed lunch and put down for a nap. Then she would have free time to do what she wanted under the king or the guards' watchful eyes, which usually resulted in her just staring at the wall. Karin would finish the day by being fed dinner and then Korrev would fuck her until she fell asleep from sheer exhaustion.

Karin wanted to say she hated when he fucked her, but to be honest, he was a good lover in bed. She hadn't had multiple one-night stands or boyfriends when she had been on Earth, but she could still tell the difference about what made a man good in bed.

Korrev always made sure she had multiple orgasms, usually one after the other, until her legs were trembling and she felt like she was out of breath. Every inch of her body had been in his mouth at some point. She was embarrassed to admit she could feel herself getting wet by simply looking at him.

She was afraid she was going to get pregnant sooner, rather than later, but she had no way of denying him. Karin had tried once, and the only thing she had managed to accomplish was to get her ass welted with his belt. Then she had been bent over the bed and fucked from behind while her sore nates had slapped against his muscular chest. Karin had never tried to deny him again.

Korrev kept a tight leash on her, literally. She learned quickly, if she didn't want to be spanked and end up with a sore, red bottom for days, she needed to do as she was told, even if it was killing her on the inside.

Karin was miserable. Everyone who looked at her could easily tell. She was pale and had lost weight. She was no longer vain when it came to her appearance like she'd once been.

Truth be told, Korrev missed her fighting spirit from earlier.

He had broken her, that part was true, but it was no longer fun like he had anticipated. Why would he want a pet who didn't play or fight back?

Plus, he hated to admit it, but he was getting worried about her. He wasn't as heartless as he pretended to be. He had grown rather fond of his pet, and it would be a hassle to break in another one.

"Karin, come," he ordered, holding her pink leash in his hand.

Karin had been sulking while staring out the window. She no longer grew shy when it came to her nakedness, with the exception of when they were with other people. This pleased Korrev. Her body was much too gorgeous to have it hidden.

Karin no longer asked him where they were going. She would just show him her neck so he could attached the leash. She knew she was not going to get an answer.

They walked in silence until they reached a familiar door, then she stiffened. She recognized it almost immediately. It was one of the healer's rooms, where Azis, one of the main healers, had already run several long, invasive and embarrassing tests on her.

"Your Majesty." Azis gave a small bow when he saw them. "I wasn't expecting you today. How may I help you?"

Korrev gave her a lazy push in the healer's direction. "She's here for a monthly check-up."

It had only been two weeks since her last monthly check-up, but of course, neither of them said anything. Instead, Azis guided Karin to lie on the long, square metal table which could be lifted up so he could view every nook and cranny with just a simple push of a button.

The check-up was fairly quick, since her last one had been so recent. Karin had seen so much of Azis, they had grown comfortable with each other's presence. After he checked her temperature, weighed her, and placed some ointment on the faded bruises on her bottom, he declared her perfectly healthy. Though Karin wasn't too happy with the suppository he had placed inside her bottom which would make her feel sleepy in about an hour.

"Karin, wait for me outside," Korrev ordered.

She looked surprised. This was the first time she had been left alone, without him watching her every move. He wasn't worried, however. If she tried to run, which he doubted, there would be guards after her before she managed to escape. Not to mention, there was a tracker on her collar.

"Your Majesty?" Azis shifted nervously. "Is something wrong?"

"I believe something is wrong with my pet."

"She lost a little weight and she seems more tired than usual, but nothing to be concerned about." He paused. "You might try to feed her her favorite foods and you could stop breeding her constantly. Humans do not have the same stamina as us. Her womanhood is swollen from you constantly being buried inside her. A cool washcloth between her legs and a nap might be all she needs to return to her old self."

"She hasn't been her old self for quite some time," Korrev insisted crabbily.

He couldn't help but think about Kyvan's mother, who had also been human. Kyvan didn't speak about her much, not because the topic was painful, but because there wasn't much to discuss.

His mother had suffered from deep sadness after his birth. Out of pity, Kyvan's father had killed her quickly so she no longer suffered. It wouldn't have been beneficial to send her back to Earth after she knew too much of their world.

Korrev would hate to do that to Karin. Even as a kindness.

She was too intelligent. Too beautiful to waste with something as common as death. He needed to fix her by whatever means necessary.

Azis hesitated. He had always been nervous about Korrev's temper which he had inherited from his father, who hadn't been an emotionally stable king.

"Speak, Azis!"

"She might also benefit from being among other females," he

replied slowly. "Humans are social creatures. Particularly females. Perhaps her mood will improve if she is given time to socialize with someone other than yourself, Your Majesty."

He nodded. Some of his warriors had taken mates, but not all. He doubted they would be happy to have their mates interact with Karin, for fear they would be corrupted by her, but no matter, he would force them to accept her.

Korrev didn't bother thanking Azis for his suggestion as he exited the room.

Karin was outside like he had instructed her, her back against the wall. She was talking to Kyvan. Though it seemed like Kyvan was doing most of the talking.

He had recently gotten a new mate, a reward for his hard work. Alice or Ali or something was her name, Korrev could never remember because, quite frankly, he didn't care. Ever since then, Kyvan had been practically bursting with joy.

Kyvan was extremely happy with his new mate, which made Korrev a little jealous. Why couldn't things have been easy for him and Karin?

He also felt a wave of irritation when he saw Karin smiling at him. Kyvan was nicer than he was, which was why most men preferred him, but Karin was his pet. She shouldn't be smiling at him like that.

Korrev gripped her leash. She stiffened. He tried to soothe her by patting her blonde hair. It didn't work.

"Karin, go back to my room," he instructed her. Karin looked surprised. This was the first time he had given her any type of freedom. She didn't question it and left immediately, the soft globes of her ass bouncing as she scurried away like a frightened animal.

He turned back to Kyvan, who looked slightly amused. "How are things proceeding with your new mate?"

"Alice is enchanting." He had a rare smile on his face. "I never knew how much a mate would change my life for the better. If I had, I would have gotten one sooner. She's napping now, but I should probably return soon."

"Before you do, I must ask if you think she'll be a good play-mate to Karin." Kyvan blinked as Korrev stared back at him cooly. "Azis suggested she might do better with a bit of socialization. Alice and Karin should have some time set aside so they can play together, which, apparently, is important to human females."

Kyvan hesitated. It was clear he wanted to keep Alice all to himself, but he would never defy him. "I suppose it will be all right."

"Excellent. We shall plan for it to happen in a few days' time."

Six

"You're staying here this morning."

Karin looked up from where she was finishing her breakfast. When he wasn't feeding her by hand, her dictator expected her to feed herself from a bowl. She was still struggling with his ill-treatment, but at least she was no longer spilling food on herself.

This was surprising news, as he often forced her to follow him everywhere until it was time for lunch and her daily nap.

"I have guests coming over to sign a treaty," he simply said as he finished drinking his drink from a nearby goblet. "It's better if they do not see you. I can't have you there. You are too distracting to me."

He would often spend his time between meetings fondling her body. As much as she wanted to be annoyed with him doing that, she had to admit that at least he brought her to orgasm every time.

Oftentimes, Karin felt like a hypocrite. She wanted to hate him for kidnapping her and forcing her to be his pet, but at the same time, it was hard to deny the way he made her feel when he had his hands on her body.

She blamed her lack of sexual experience on the way her traitorous body would grow wet whenever he even looked in her direction.

Karin tried to hide the giddiness in her voice. This could be the perfect chance for her to escape. She wasn't quite sure where she would escape to, exactly, but she also knew as soon as she was no longer inside the palace walls, she had a greater chance of freedom. Karin could worry about how she would get to Earth later. All she needed was to be away from Korrev.

"I'll be back by the midday meal and to put you down for a nap," he warned.

She tried to hide her disappointment. It was still plenty of time, so she shouldn't fret. "I understand."

Korrev nodded as he motioned her to follow him back to the bedroom. They'd just had sex this morning and she wasn't sure if she would have the energy to continue their lovemaking,

Much to her surprise, instead, he pulled out a small bottle and black butt plug from the drawer right next to his bed.

Korrev smiled when he saw her most bewildered expression. "You humans have the most delightful inventions. Bend over my knee, Karin. Now."

Karin didn't move. She couldn't. It was too embarrassing to drape herself over the knee of her kidnapper so he could insert a butt plug in her ass because he didn't trust her to behave. She didn't need a reminder. She was a grown woman!

"Karin!" Korrev's voice was sharp. "Get over my knee. Now!"

Karin's eyes started burning, which meant she was close to crying, but she wouldn't cry. Not again. Not for him. Not for anyone.

"Do you want another session with my belt?" he asked her quietly.

She shivered. She hated being spanked with his belt. There was nothing worse, except perhaps the bath brush which he used on her bare, wet bottom if she misbehaved during a bath.

"No," she whined.

"Then be a good girl and get over my knee."

Karin moved her feet. She didn't want a butt plug, and perhaps she could fight a bit harder, but the truth of the matter was she didn't want a spanking.

She draped herself over his knee. Karin immediately felt something warm fall on the top of her bottom cheeks.

"Spread your cheeks."

With trembling hands, Karin reached back and pulled her ass cheeks wide open. Her other cheeks flushed bright red at the image she surely must be presenting. Korrev could see everything. Her pussy, her ass, and now her tight, bottom hole which would soon be stretched by the plug.

He had seen it before, of course, when he was fucking her from behind, but now he was viewing it much more closely. Especially with how it was twitching in fear.

"Relax," Korrev scolded her quietly as he covered her hole with the warm liquid which seemed slippery and thicker than lube. "It won't go in if you're tense."

"I don't want it to go in at all!"

"Having the plug in you will make you behave." Korrev's fingers caressed her tight rosebud, trying to cover every inch of her with lube. "Not to mention, it will stretch you and get you ready to accept my cock."

Karin paled at the idea of having to accept his cock in her ass. She could barely accept it in her pussy. She always felt sore afterwards for days, she couldn't imagine how her ass would feel afterwards if he ended up fucking her there.

Korrev didn't warn her when the butt plug was slowly inserted inside her. It wasn't big, but she had never had something shoved up there before. She tried to move away, but his thick leg over the back of her knees kept her in place.

"Please." She gritted her teeth. "It hurts. It's too big."

He gave her ass a light slap. "It's not big at all. Just relax."

Korrev pushed the plug in slowly, ignoring her cries of protest as her ass swallowed the base of the plug until it was fully inside her.

A tear or two managed to escape despite trying to hold it in. Korrev helped her up, then wiped the loose tears with the back of his thumb. "Have I broken you already?" The bastard almost sounded disappointed.

"You will never break me!" Karin said, even though it would be better for her in the long run if she learned to keep her mouth shut.

He chuckled instead of scolding her. "We'll see. Stay inside. I'll give you a treat later if you behave."

Karin allowed herself to burst into tears the second he left. After she pitied herself for a good while, she went to inspect her butt in the mirror. This was one of the rare occasions when her ass wasn't bright red. It was barely pink and the marks of her last punishment would soon fade. She refused to get excited, though. The ability to sit never lasted long. The king loved to punish her too much.

Seated between her two bare cheeks, was a black plug which caused her entire body to flush red with embarrassment. Oh, she hated him! She hated him so much! Karin would not stand for this. This was just one humiliation too many. She would not spend the rest of her life as a pet.

Then Karin realized something marvelous. She was alone.

Korrev hadn't placed her in a cage or tied her to a bedpost. He hadn't locked her in, either. She was gloriously alone.

Maybe he was testing her. She chewed on her bottom lip. Or maybe he had simply forgotten.

Whatever the case might be, it didn't matter. This was her one chance of escape, to finally be free.

Karin was torn. If she did escape, she was certain she would find a way to get to freedom or at least far away from the palace.

If she didn't, well, she didn't want to think of the consequences. But Karin Johansson had never considered herself a coward or a submissive. She wasn't about to start now. She said a quick prayer even though she wasn't particularly religious, and then she made her move.

Karin had barely been running for five minutes when someone recognized her. A guard or warrior, she wasn't sure, but they yelled, "Pet! What are you doing outside without the king?"

Maybe they recognized her blonde hair or the pink bow around her neck. It didn't matter. Karin just started to run until she felt her heart was threatening to jump out of her chest and until the soles of her feet hurt.

She might not be the strongest person in Krotev, but she was fast. Her smaller stature actually helped her evade what seemed like the many guards who were after her. She just needed to lose them and then she would be able to come up with a much better plan. At least, she hoped so.

Karin breathed a sigh of relief when she saw a door handle in what seemed like an endless hallway. Her hand gripped the doorknob and she turned it, stepping inside.

Her relief was short-lived, however, when she realized the room she had entered was the same room where the king was having his unexpected meeting.

He was standing at the head of the table, of course, having a drink with a man on either side, though she supposed using the word "man" might be generous. One of Korrev's guests was bright blue, with what looked like slimy tentacles for arms.

The other one, across from him, was a bright magenta color, with thin-looking lips. Neither of them were particularly pleasant-looking. She was suddenly glad Korrev, at least, had the ability to transform himself between his human and alien form.

The blue alien gave her a smile. "Now, who is this, Korrev? Have you brought a treat for us?" He looked at her bare thighs. "She is quite pleasant-looking."

She shielded her breasts, suddenly feeling very naked.

"Is she human?" The magenta alien blinked curiously, as if she were an exotic fish at the aquarium. "I know Krotev is filled with them, with all the breeding you seem to do, but I've never seen one up close before. They are rather pleasant-looking. Very soft."

Karin looked at Korrev, expecting him to yell before placing her over his knee. He had given her strict orders to stay where she belonged after all.

"Bick, Toli, this is my pet." There was a slight edge to Korrev's voice, which she did not like at all. "Karin. She is human, and as you can see, she is very naughty. Humans are not very good at following directions. They all have that terrible fighting spirit, I'm afraid."

The magenta alien, which she guessed was named Bick, let out a laugh. "That makes it all the more fun, Korrev. No one wants a dolt who just follows your every command."

"Perhaps." Korrev's voice was cold. He was only staring at Karin, which made a shiver go down her spine. "What are you doing here, Pet? I told you to stay in our bedroom. You are being very naughty."

Before she could come up with a lie, one of the guards threw the door open, looking out of breath. "Your Majesty! We are terribly sorry. Shall we escort your pet back to your quarters?"

"No, leave us." Korrev looked at Bick and Toli. "I apologize, but we must reschedule our meeting for later this evening, once I put my pet down for a very early bedtime. A feast has been prepared for your enjoyment. Please start without me."

Both Bick and Toli looked disappointed but didn't argue. She almost begged them to take her with them.

As soon as the two aliens had left, Korrev pounced on her like a hungry animal. It terrified her how furious he could get, as if he could break every bone in her body in just a quick second. This made her extremely nervous.

"What are you doing here, Pet?" He gave her a cold smile as he ran a finger down her cheek. "You were supposed to stay in our room."

"I wanted to see you," she lied pathetically.

"Liar." He smirked as he rubbed her clavicle with his index finger. "I could hear my warriors screaming about an escaped pet. You might be fast, Karin, but not fast enough for me. Do you know why I didn't want you at this meeting?"

She shook her head slowly.

"Because my men know how to keep their hands to themselves. They know you belong to me." He narrowed his eyes. "These men, however, don't. Do you think I wanted them to see you like this?" He looked at her curvy figure.

"It's not my fault you don't let me wear any clothes!" Karin hissed in return when, in reality, she should have been keeping her mouth shut.

"You were supposed to stay inside." He gripped her wrist. "You sent my men on a wild chase that will not be tolerated."

Tears burned in her eyes. "Nothing will ever be good enough for you."

"All I'm asking for, sweet pet, is for you to obey." He led her down to one of the couches and forced her down on her knees until her butt was sticking out.

Karin stiffened, preparing herself for a whipping. She didn't bother running. There wasn't anywhere where she could escape from Korrev.

Much to her surprise, she didn't feel an implement or his hand on her ass. Instead, she felt warm liquid dripping down her cheeks and down the crack of her ass.

"No!" she squeaked, instantly realizing what was happening. She tried to squirm, but he was grabbing her by the waist. "Please, no!"

He chuckled darkly. "Oh, Pet, don't start begging now. This

is only part one of your punishment. It seems I need to remind you what happens to bad little pets who don't obey." He touched the butt plug in her ass. She moaned. "At least you were a good little girl and kept this in."

"Please, Korrev. I am not ready."

"Oh, I will make you ready, Pet. I will even be gentle."

He pulled out the plug from her bottom and she whimpered for what was about to come next.

"Please, Korrev. Don't do this."

He started rubbing the back of her head in an almost affectionate manner, but it quite frankly felt like he was making fun of her. "Then you shouldn't have misbehaved. I warned you from the beginning. You embarrassed me, Pet. My guests might think I cannot control my pet. You've earned this. I hope you remember that."

She didn't bother pulling away. She knew it would be worse for her if she did. He could easily catch her. Karin just needed to take her punishment, even if she was sure she would cry during the entire ordeal.

He parted her cheeks open with much more gentleness than she had anticipated. Perhaps he wouldn't be as cruel as she had feared.

"Relax your cheeks." He gave her bottom a light slap. "Even your hole is trembling."

"Well, your cock is not exactly small," she couldn't help but mumble as she forced herself to relax.

He laughed, sounding less angry than he had earlier. Korrev started rubbing some of the warm liquid on her anus, making sure he covered every inch of her. Once or twice, he would insert the tip of one of his fingers, which would cause her to rock her hips to the motion of his fingers.

She would be lying if she said his fingers didn't feel good in her ass, but it didn't mean she wanted his cock to impale her.

Karin stiffened when she felt him remove his fingers for the third time. Then she felt something slippery and stiff touching her anus. His cock.

Her whole body started trembling, even though his anger had subsided from earlier.

"Relax, Karin," he murmured in her ear as he stroked her neck with his fingers. "Be a good girl and take your punishment."

Be a good girl. She so wanted to be a good girl, even though she was a thirty-something year old woman. Deep down, she wanted to make Korrev happy, and to be honest, she didn't even know why, which seemed to confuse her even more.

Korrev slowly pushed in, instead of slamming into her as she had anticipated. When his tip finally entered her, her knees buckled. Korrev gripped her by the hips and started pushing into her slowly, parting her open.

She whimpered but didn't move. At least not as much as she wanted to.

Korrev rewarded her with a kiss to the back of her head. He started parting her back hole slowly with his large cock. Karin felt like she was being spread in half by his big dick. Even though she felt like there wasn't any more space for him, he somehow managed to continue to fill her.

Despite the pain of being impaled by his manhood, she also felt something different and strange. It was hard to describe the feeling. The best word she could use to describe it was exhilaration. She was torn between wanting the whole process to stop and to see if his cock truly fit inside her small body.

"You're doing very well, my good girl." Korrev's anger seemed to have diminished for now. His fingers found her terribly swollen clit and he started rubbing it slowly until it was the only thing Karin could focus on instead of her punishment.

She let out a small, "Oh!" as his balls hit the backs of her thighs. She suddenly felt very full and very wet. Karin could feel her entire face grow hot. He was fully inside her right now.

King Korrev had claimed her in every way he could. In her pussy. In her mouth. And now, in her ass.

Karin's eyes welled up with tears. It was a mixture of shame and arousal. She had vowed she would fight him back. Instead, she had allowed him to claim every part of her. Hell, she sometimes even lusted after him like a cat in heat.

"You're being good, Pet. No need for tears. At least not yet." Before she could even ask what he meant by that, he pulled out of her, only to slam into her once again.

"Oh!" Karin squealed as he pumped into her, not as harshly as the first time but still roughly.

Korrev grabbed each of her thighs and lifted her up as he fucked her slowly, making sure she felt every inch of him filling her insides.

"You are never to disobey me in public, especially in front of my guests. Is that understood, Pet?" he asked.

"Yes!" Karin moaned as he pinched her clit between two fingers at the same time as he filled her completely once again.

Korrev finished inside her almost immediately. Karin lay limply on the couch as she felt his hot seed drip out of her. Her face was flushed and she felt extremely tired. The only thing she wanted to do was crawl into bed, but she had a feeling Korrev wouldn't let her go anytime soon.

Korrev slapped her ass as he let her go. Karin fell on the couch face first, with her butt in the air, as she waited to catch her breath. She felt tired, swollen, and sweaty. She hoped this was the end of her punishment. She didn't know how much of this she could take.

The king let her rest for a few minutes, but he soon grew impatient. He helped her up and she winced when she felt the soreness between her cheeks. "Let's go back to the bedroom."

"Don't you need to return to your guests?"

He gave her a wolfish smile. "They will be okay without me

for an hour. Believe me, we aren't done with your punishment for this little stunt you pulled."

Her eyes widened. "Oh, please, Korrev. No more. I am so sore."

"Shush. I decide when your punishment ends. Not you." He opened the door, even though cum was still dripping out of her. "Now, walk."

Seven

Karin would be lying if she said she wasn't trembling with nervousness as she went back to their bedroom with the king hot on her heels, no doubt watching the way the soft globes on her ass gently bounced.

She almost wished he would just whip her ass and get her punishment over with. The anticipation seemed much worse than the actual punishment. At least, with a spanking, she knew eventually it would be over and she would be allowed to cry herself to sleep.

When Korrev gave her more creative punishments, she wasn't sure when they would end. She liked it much better when he would just stick to the spankings, but it seemed he wasn't heading in that direction this time.

Her outer and inner ass felt sore and she felt her bottom hole twitch with each movement. She still couldn't believe he had fucked her in the ass while she was bent over and he hadn't been at all gentle, even though he had known it was her first time.

Korrev had taken her roughly and aggressively, but not enough to really hurt her. She had been stupid to think he would ever be gentle, especially in the bedroom.

He was a warrior, a king. Sex, for him, was just another way to showcase his sexist, pigheaded nature.

Despite the fact she was sore, Karin would be lying if she said she hadn't gotten a bit wet. Even now, as she was walking, she could feel the wetness which had dripped from her pussy and now covered her inner thighs.

Damn it! Her body wasn't supposed to react like this. She was a modern woman for God's sakes.

If she were back on Earth, she would have sued his ass a thousand times and have him thrown in jail. But she wasn't on Earth. She was in Krotev, and she was at his mercy.

She hoped Korrev didn't notice how much her body ached for him despite his behavior, but who was she kidding? Korrev noticed. He always did.

When they finally made it to the bedroom, Karin sucked in her cheeks and forced herself to turn around. "Well?" she demanded bravely. "If you're going to punish me, do it now."

Korrev gave her a cold smile. "You don't make the rules, Pet. I do." For a few minutes, he didn't say anything, which only seemed to make her more nervous. Her blue eyes followed him as he opened the large window facing the garden.

One of the trees had grown so much in the past few months, it was nearly pushing itself against the window. Yet Korrev had never asked one of the servants to cut it. She had never minded, because she had thought it was pretty.

"Pick a switch," he ordered calmly.

"A what?"

"A switch. It's a thin branch from a tree. Pick one. Now. Before I do it for you. Make sure it does not have any leaves or any splinters. I don't want to make you bleed."

She hesitated, before meekly approaching the window. The tree had grown so much, the branches were nearly poking her eyes out.

Karin had heard of being spanked with a switch, but never in a million years, did she ever think, as a grown woman, she would be picking her own switch.

"I'm waiting, Karin."

She fought the urge to glare at him. Her inner ass was already sore enough and she had a bad feeling her outer ass would soon follow. She could pick a small branch and hope the king would take pity on her, but who was she kidding?

The king never took pity on anyone, let alone her. He might make her pick a larger branch, just to spite her. Instead, she picked a medium-sized one.

"Good girl," he said as he took the branch from her. "Stand up straight, legs apart, facing forward. I am going to strike you wherever I see fit. If you attempt to jump out of the way, you will receive an additional lash. If you attempt to cover yourself, you will also receive another lash. Understand?"

"How many am I getting?"

"Twenty-five. Are you ready?"

What else was she supposed to say? But she kept the bitterness to herself as she allowed herself to nod.

Thwack!

The first switch landed in the center of her plump breasts, covering both of them easily. He left behind a pale pink mark just below her throbbing pink nipples. Even while she was punished, her nipples were fully erect and hard, something which was hard to ignore even though Korrev didn't say anything.

Thwack!

The second switch landed just underneath the curve of her breasts which caused her to jump and for her breasts to bounce slightly. Korrev didn't say anything as six more switch marks landed on her breasts, covering her chest with long, bright pink switch marks with an assortment of welts.

Tears pooled in her eyes. Karin didn't even bother vowing she wouldn't cry. She always tried not to, but Korrev had the ability to reduce her to tears within minutes. It didn't help that he had just anal fucked her for the first time for being disobedient.

Her boobs burned and felt heavy, or it might have been because her breasts were becoming swollen because of the switch marks. Her toes curled as she jumped from side to side.

Korrev didn't say anything until he missed her.

He raised a pale eyebrow. "One."

Before she could ask what it meant, Karin felt the switch being slapped against the center on her pussy, hitting her poor clit.

Karin yelped as she moved her hips, as if that would get rid of the sting.

"Don't move again, Karin."

Tears burned her eyes as she bit her lip. Her poor breasts and nipples felt incredibly sore.

Korrev ignored her breasts and focused on her round ass.

Thwack!

Thwack!

Thwack!

He landed the switch three times on her ass, leaving behind several matching pink marks on her plump ass cheeks. Her round ass bounced against the switch lewdly and her breasts bounced against each other with each stroke.

Tears poured down her face and landed on her chest. She felt incredibly sore. Her body ached. She hated being spanked. It made her feel so small and insignificant.

"Please," Karin blubbered. "I'm sorry; I won't ever do it again."

She didn't think he would stop, but he did. He threw the switch on the floor. "Come here," he said simply.

Karin did as she was told, burying her face against his chest. She cried as if her heart was breaking.

Korrev shushed her as he rubbed her back and bottom until

he soothed her crying. He led her to the bathroom and filled the tub with warm water and soothing bath salts. Then he helped her into the tub. She whimpered as her sore cheeks touched the water.

Neither of them said anything as Korrev bathed her silently, making sure he was gentle when he touched her switch marks.

She hated him. Oh, how she hated him. If Karin weren't so weak, she would make him pay for his humiliation.

He dried her slowly. "I'm going to put you to bed," he said simply. "No lunch for you."

Karin didn't say anything as he dried her hair. She was going to give him the silent treatment until he apologized for treating her so cruelly.

Korrev wasn't one to apologize, but it seemed he hadn't realized how stubborn Karin could be as well.

The days passed slowly. Karin continued giving him the silent treatment, not caring how childish she looked. Korrev was stubborn, but Karin was more.

She was tired of being punished and being treated like a bad little pet, when all she wanted was to go back to Earth or at least be thought of as Korrev's equal. Not that it was ever going to happen under Korrev's rule, but she could at least try.

For three days, she ignored Korrev. During dinner, she ate the food she was offered silently. During bath times, she refused to utter a sound, even when his hands would go between her thighs. She refused to sleep in his bed when he tried to coax her, even though his large bed was much more comfortable than hers.

By the fourth day, he was clearly losing his patience and he placed Karin over his knee while he spanked her with a small wooden paddle. He punished her until her poor, wobbling cheeks were a berry red color. A few tears had escaped from her eyes, but never a wail or a begging word and she was proud of herself.

This was currently the fifth day, and Korrev was obviously angry because he hadn't been able to make her have a conversation with him, which made her secretly thrilled.

Karin had spent the entire morning in the throne room while Korrev listened to the boring reports given to him about what was happening in the kingdom. In a rare moment of kindness, Korrev had her pet bed placed next to him on the throne so she could lie down on her belly instead of her back.

Karin could tell Korrev was in a bad mood because of the announcements he had heard today. There was some unrest in southern Krotev, and some of the peace treaties with the other planets hadn't been going well.

"Go!" he ordered the oddly scrawny alien in front of her, who was in charge of giving the report.

Karin would have laughed if she wasn't feeling so sore. Usually, it was just her butt and the backs of her thighs, but today, it was also her breasts. The switch marks were healing which made her boobs feel itchy. Both of them were feeling crabby.

Korrev cursed under his breath for several minutes about everyone's incompetence. Then before she knew it, he started removing his clothes right in the throne room.

Karin had seen him nude plenty of times, but she always became a bit embarrassed when she saw him. Especially in public. Korrev had an amazing body. It would be foolish for her not to agree.

He trained for hours. Usually with Kyvan, but sometimes with the others. Karin was sometimes allowed to see, when he wasn't instructing her to nap. His body was all muscle and hard as a rock. Every part of him was. Even when he was spanking her, she could feel his heavy hand slapping down on her ass.

If he was removing his clothes, it meant he was going to fuck her again, probably in the throne room.

She had never fucked him here before. Karin hoped it was soundproof.

He sat down again, then pointed to his erect member.

She blushed. Why was he always hard? Didn't he ever get tired?

"Suck." Korrev rested his back against the throne. "Get on your knees and suck, Karin."

"You could at least say please," Karin grumbled under her breath as she got down on her knees. She placed his cock inside her mouth and began to please him. Karin sucked him, her cheeks becoming hollow as she did while she glared at him angrily, silently cursing him.

The bastard had the audacity to smirk at her as he placed a hand on the back of her head.

His cock felt heavy in her mouth and she was having a hard time taking it all in. She flinched when she heard someone open the door. Oh, no, she couldn't have someone see her in this position. It was too embarrassing!

She tried to pull back, but Korrev refused to allow her to move from this position. "Suck." He narrowed his eyes at her. "Unless you want me to use your other entrance with only spit as lubricant."

Tears filled her eyes. She wanted to defy him, but she also knew he was in such a foul mood, he would follow up on his threat. So, Karin continued sucking him off until she felt her jaw ache.

Korrev's tone softened as he stroked her blonde hair. "Good choice, Karin." Then, in a much different type of voice, he said, "Stop. Come forward."

She did as she was told with his cock still in her mouth. It was hard to just breathe with her nose, but she didn't want to displease him. Karin also didn't want to turn around. It was embarrassing being in this position, even though everyone had gotten used to her being the king's pet.

"Unless you want to be in the same place as my Karin is right now." A cruel smirk was on the king's face.

Her eyes watered with tears. Was that how he saw her? Only as someone who had to do as she was told? Who was only good at breeding babies and warming his bed at night? Of course, it was how he saw her. It wasn't like he had picked her for future intellectual conversations. Still, did he have to make her feel like such a tramp?

"Turn around," he ordered briskly.

Karin assumed it wasn't one of his warriors or one of the palace staff, because he knew all of them by name. It must be a mate. Karin felt slightly better. A mate was used to being humiliated, though probably not publicly like her.

She let out a little whining sound, to let him know she was tired of having his cock in her mouth. He released her even though he was not done coming.

Karin used the back of her hand to dry her lips, then she turned towards the girl in front of her. She was young, probably in her early twenties, with long, thick, coal-black hair, pale skin, and blue eyes.

Unlike her and every other mate out there, she was not naked. She was actually wearing a blue dress which barely covered her rump. She was exposing her cheeks to Korrev while her face blushed red with shame.

A blue collar was around her neck with a bow. Blue. The same shade as her eyes.

Even though she was bent down, she had a determined look in her eyes, although her entire body was trembling. She couldn't help but think Korrev would probably be able to crush her spirit like he had done to her.

"Stand up. You're Kyvan's brat, I figure. I would have thought he would have a tighter hold on you."

Kyvan? The king's best friend? She had only seen him a couple of times. He was polite to her but kept his distance.

Korrev had mentioned in passing he had given him a mate. It was odd she was facing her now.

"I didn't expect her to be so mischievous." Kyvan came into the room, looking both annoyed and embarrassed that he couldn't control Alice. He gripped her wrist, and Karin winced.

Korrev led Karin to lay her head on his thigh. He didn't seem to be embarrassed by his nakedness and she was too tired to care. It felt like the past few days, she had either spent it getting punished or lying on her punished backside while he fucked her.

"Keep her on a tighter leash, Kyvan. I don't like being interrupted."

Karin watched sleepily as Alice and Kyvan bickered. Once they left, she turned to look at him. "Do you want me to continue to please you?"

"No." Korrev gently pulled her up and started dressing himself. "You look overtired. I'm going to put you down for a nap. It looks like you haven't been sleeping."

"And whose fault is that?" she quipped.

Korrev didn't deny this, nor did he apologize. She expected him to put her on a leash like he often did when he wasn't happy with her, but instead, he picked her up and placed her over this thick, heavy shoulder.

He sometimes did this, but only when she was being naughty. It was odd he was doing it now.

Karin didn't complain. Instead, she focused on the way his hand touched the back of her thighs and the way he protectively held her so she wouldn't fall.

Eight

"What did you want to discuss?" Kyvan asked as he stretched his muscles. Korrev had asked him to meet him after he put down Karin for her daily nap after lunch.

"Alice."

Kyvan looked surprised. No doubt, he had been expecting to discuss something in regards to treaty or battle. His mood darkened, his protective side coming out. Korrev had made it clear he didn't like his little mate, and therefore, he was now being protective of her.

"What about her?" he asked tensely.

"I want to move forward with what we discussed previously," he said calmly. "About providing Karin with a playdate. I'm assuming Alice gets lonely from time to time."

"I suppose so," he said uncomfortably.

Alice had a temper, and Kyvan sometimes struggled to control her. Korrev had advised him to take a belt to her ass more often, something which he had obviously not agreed upon. No wonder Alice had him wrapped around her little finger.

She wasn't exactly his first choice as a friend for Karin, especially since his other warriors had much nicer, better controlled mates. Still, the only warrior he truly trusted like a brother was Kyvan, which meant he had to deal with Alice.

"Good. So, you'll bring her the day after tomorrow." It wasn't a question. "Bring her before lunch, to my private gardens. I don't like Karin's schedule to change too much."

Kyvan bowed, and his jaw tensed. It was clear he was unhappy letting Alice out of his sight. Especially since Karin hadn't been a model pet, either, but he didn't have a choice. Korrev was the king, and the king gave orders.

On the day of the appointed playdate, Korrev found Karin playing with one of his old, complicated puzzles from his childhood which had been used to test endurance, perseverance, and patience.

She grew bored sitting around all day or following him around when he had errands or meetings to run. Karin had found this box of puzzles when she had been cleaning and had quickly become enamored by an activity which made her "think more".

"Get up, Karin," he instructed.

"Do you have another meeting?" she asked with a pout as she left behind her puzzle. Usually, he only brought her to meetings to show off her beauty. Karin had made it clear on more than one occasion that she grew tired of being paraded around like a "show pony", whatever that meant.

"No. You have a playdate." He let her out of his quarters with, thankfully, no pink leash in his hand.

Karin looked surprised. "With whom?"

Karin didn't seem like a very sociable creature compared to the other females. He was actually surprised she didn't refuse to go. She was older than most of the younger mates and much too serious sometimes for Korrev's liking. He hoped Alice's immaturity would rub off on her.

"Alice. Kyvan's mate."

She paled, then looked embarrassed. "The girl who stormed in when I was on my knees," she blushed, and Korrev smirked, "the one with the blue bow."

"Yes." Korrev placed a hand gently on her lower back once they reached his private gardens. "You have nothing to be ashamed about. Believe me, Alice has had her own share of punishments."

"Is she nice?" Karin hesitated, sounding younger than she was. It was like she was worried Alice would tease her for her low status of being a king's pet.

"If she isn't, you will tell me and I will deal with her," Korrev responded curtly.

Karin was taken to the private gardens of the king, this time without a leash, to wait for their guests.

Korrev could tell she was nervous, by the way she kept squirming and looking over her shoulder. He finally had to tell her to kneel down next to him and be quiet. She complied but was obviously embarrassed by her nudity.

Korrev wondered if this was a good idea, but Azis had told him she might be happier if she had a friend to play with. To be quite honest, he didn't trust anyone but Kyvan, even if his mate was questionable.

Deep down, he wanted Karin to be happy, not just an empty shell who obeyed his every command. If it meant he had to order somebody to be her friend, so be it.

Finally, Kyvan arrived, tugging a pouty-looking Alice behind. Alice had long, black hair and sparkling blue eyes. She had squeezed herself into a short blue dress which barely covered her rump.

"You're late," Korrev snapped.

"I apologize." Kyvan squeezed Alice's hip, looking amused. He was the only one of his warriors not afraid of him. "She insisted on a dress."

Korrev shook his head in disgust. "You're spoiling her." He

tilted his chin towards the garden. "You two go play. We have to talk."

Karin hesitated a bit before she motioned Alice to follow her towards the gardens, which were filled with fruit trees.

Korrev and Kyvan talked easily about their prospective mates and their breeding attempts before he told his friend it was time he put his pet down for a nap.

Korrev snapped his fingers at Karin.

Karin went to him almost instantly. He smiled at her obedience as he squeezed her hip. "Good girl," he murmured in her ear. "You are going to get a reward later."

Karin smiled mysteriously.

"Did you girls have fun?" Kyvan pressed his lips against Alice's forehead, none the wiser.

Alice nodded.

"Wonderful, perhaps we can do this again sometime. You girls need someone to talk to, don't you, since you're always cooped up inside?" Kyvan looked at Korrev, who nodded at his request as he squeezed one of Karin's plump buttocks, not caring about them standing there.

"I don't want to leave," Alice whined.

Korrev pushed Karin towards his chest in a rare moment of public affection. At least his pet wasn't the one throwing a tantrum this time.

"Alice," Kyvan gave her a warning, his eyes glaring down on her, indicating he was close to losing his patience. "You and Karin can play another time. For now, we have to go home."

Alice didn't seem to agree as she stubbornly refused to move. Korrev couldn't help but chuckle. His friend certainly had his hands full.

Kyvan finally got tired of her tantrums and placed a struggling Alice over his shoulder before dragging her back to his quarters.

Once Alice and Kyvan left bickering, Korrev turned back to

Karin. "Let's go eat lunch and then I'll place you down for your nap."

Usually, after lunch, Korrev would place Karin down for a nap and then go do things he couldn't get done when she was alert and awake. This time, however, he surprised himself and Karin when he willingly lay down in her pet bed beside her, even if the tiny bed was too small for his seven-foot body.

Karin had gotten used to him by now, so she no longer flinched when he would press her body against him. In fact, she would willingly seek his warm body, especially when she was sleepy.

"Did you have fun today?" he asked as he stroked her blonde hair away from her face.

"I did," she agreed sleepily. "This was my first playdate."

"It was?" Korrev sounded surprised. Humans, from his perspective were usually very sociable. Especially females.

"Yes." Karin yawned. "I never had friends growing up. Then I went to law school where friendships didn't exist because competition was so fierce."

"Did you like Alice? I know she's quite a bit younger than you."

"I like her very much. She is very sweet."

Korrev snorted. Sweet wasn't the word he would use to describe her.

"Is Kyvan your best friend?"

"I suppose so." Korrev didn't have time to ponder over the idea of friends. "He's been with me since we were boys. He's my second in command and the one I trust above others. Which is why I gifted him Alice. He has proven his loyalty throughout the decades and he deserves to be rewarded."

Karin chuckled sleepily. "You give awful presents."

Korrev was about to tease her back when he realized she was fast asleep. He kissed her forehead. He wasn't usually a sentimental person, but there was something about Karin which made him softer and less tense. Just a little bit.

Korrev was a loner by nature. As king, he had to be. He could never fully trust someone without worrying about betrayal. With the exception of Kyvan.

But when he was with Karin, he felt different, even when she was acting like a brat. He felt almost content. Something which he had not felt for quite some time.

Korrev wondered how he had lived so many years without her.

Nine

Karin was snuggled up against Korrev. It was one of the rare instances when he had allowed her to sleep in his bed with him instead of sleeping in her pet bed.

She wanted to hate it. She should hate it, but she secretly loved it. Karin liked being wrapped in his strong arms. When he thought she was asleep, he would sometimes pet her head or stroke her cheeks which, if she was being honest with herself, would make her shiver with glee inside.

It was in moments like these, she could almost pretend they were a real couple. She could fantasize he was another hot shot lawyer at the same company she used to work for who had somehow whisked her away to her fancy New York City penthouse.

For a few hours while she was asleep, Karin could pretend they were equals instead of being a powerful king and his pet.

Despite the unhappiness she felt because she was still trapped in Krotev months later, her bouts of depression and frustration had been less. Her punishments had lessened and Karin hadn't tried anything stupid like running away, since the last time she had failed.

Korrev had also softened towards her in his own way. He had stopped being cruel to her and his punishments weren't as harsh. Dare she say, they had become almost like an erotic game instead of an actual punishment. Karin couldn't even say she hated when he punished her anymore because she would always get wet when he did.

Perhaps one of the reasons why she had also come to accept her new life was because she had found a new friend in Alice. Despite the age difference, the two women got along well and she was a spitfire.

Back in New York, she had never been very sociable due to her work schedule, but now she had all the time in the world. It truly felt nice to have friends. It was also one of the few times when the king actually gave her privacy and wasn't hovering over her.

But even though Karin had come to accept her new way of life, a part of her still longed for the old life she had led. A life where she was independent and could make choices pertaining to her life. Where she didn't have to listen to a king who knew how to make her body scream with pleasure.

Unlike Alice, who seemed to be content staying with her mate, a part of Karin still dreamed of returning to New York. She knew she needed to return fast.

Karin had been injected with fertility treatments and Korrev never bothered using protection. It was a miracle she wasn't pregnant yet, but she couldn't take any chances. Once she became pregnant, there was no way she could return to Earth, even if she did manage to escape.

Even if Korrev didn't bother to try to get her back, there was no way Karin would be able to raise a half-alien child on Earth. Her baby would be used as a lab experiment, perhaps something worse. She wouldn't feel comfortable terminating the pregnancy, either.

No, she had to escape. Soon. Before she ended up carrying a baby she wasn't even sure she wanted.

The problem? How was Karin going to escape?

Korrev was still watching her closely, not as much as he used to, since he thought he had domesticated her, but still pretty closely.

Karin couldn't escape and fail again. She shuddered, thinking of her punishment if she was caught again. She didn't want to think about it. No, it had to be the perfect plan. She just needed to wait and pray she didn't get pregnant in the meantime.

Karin was still sleeping soundly in the king's arms when a huge blast shook her awake, along with the whole bed.

Korrev immediately went into warrior mode as he jumped out of bed. There was anger in his eyes, but this time, it was not directed at her.

"Get up!" he barked as he threw the red cape over her shoulders and wrapped it tightly around her shivering frame.

She didn't even have time to blush at his protective gesture because she was frightened. Instead, she watched as Korrev put on his heavy suit of armor and tied his blond hair in a ponytail while he told her to hurry up.

"What's going on?" she managed to ask as he dragged her down the long corridors while he barked orders at his men.

The whole palace was in a frenzy. There were guards everywhere, much more than she had ever seen before. Everyone was running in different directions. She saw mates being taken away somewhere safe, while warriors grabbed weapons which were the size of her head.

"Korrev, are we at war?"

"We are," Korrev answered tightly. "We expected it, of course, but never in the dead of night. This is a cowardly attack." He pulled her in the direction of the basement, and she had to walk down several steps.

"When will it be over? Will it take years?" She gulped, thinking of both World Wars. Aliens were much more violent than humans. What if they enjoyed war and this lasted for decades? She might be an old lady before she managed to escape.

Korrev chuckled as if she had said something amusing. "Not years, Pet. We are not amateurs. With any luck, we will be done by this afternoon and we'll be snuggled in our bed once more by nightfall."

Karin gulped. "Wow, that's fast." She didn't know if it was a good or bad thing.

"Many planets do not dare challenge Krotev." Korrev sounded proud. "They know if they do, they will not live to tell the tale of their demise."

Karin had to admit, while Korrev might be an asshole, he was actually a pretty good leader. She doubted anyone could lead the Krotev aliens into battle as successfully as he could.

"What am I doing here?" Karin shivered when he finally led her down to the basement. There was a steel cage in the center, with plenty of pillows and blankets, but it was still a cage, no matter how prettily they decorated it.

There were two warriors in their alien forms, which no longer terrified Karin, looking as if they wanted to be anywhere else but here.

"Get in the cage, Karin," he instructed her tensely.

"Why?" she whined. "I've been good. I've been doing everything you have asked me to do."

"You've been very good," he assured her as he patted her cheek. His voice had softened, but it was clear there were other things on his mind. "This is not a punishment, Pet. The cage is meant to keep you safe. I cannot fight and be worried about you. This is the safest place in the palace. If something happens, or if our enemies come into the palace, they will take you to safety." He motioned to the guards who clearly would prefer to fight instead of being forced to guard an unruly pet.

"But—"

"I do not have time to fight about this, Karin. Nor do I have time to punish you. Get in the cage." Korrev gritted his teeth with each word. "I promise, you will be rewarded if you are a good pet."

Karin didn't have any other options but to drag her feet and get into the cage her king had procured for her. She waited for Korrev to say something else, but he didn't. Instead, he just stormed out of the basement, leaving her feeling hurt while the guards mumbled under their breaths how they would prefer to be up there fighting.

The hours were long as Karin waited in the cage by herself, especially since the guards had no desire to talk to her. She didn't have anything to entertain herself with and she wished Alice could at least accompany her during this time.

Karin managed to sleep a bit, but the only thing she could think about was Korrev. Sometimes she hoped he was safe. Other times, she wished he would be killed as punishment for being such a brute to her.

Karin was surprised to realize, unlike in the beginning, she was not quite sure if she wanted him dead or not. His arms might deliver hard strokes against her bottom, but they were surprisingly warm and gentle when they wanted to be.

She wondered what would happen if Korrev died. He didn't have any heirs, which meant someone else would be king. But then, what would happen to her? She would probably be sold off again, to be someone's mate. The idea caused her to shiver with dread.

Karin didn't want another mate or master. She would rather have Korrev.

Finally, she heard the creak of a door opening, followed by heavy footsteps. The guards stopped playing a game which they played with pebbles and immediately straightened up.

Her heart was thumping inside her chest. Was it good news, or bad news?

A sigh of relief escaped from her mouth the second she saw the pale blond hair belonging to the king. His armor was destroyed and there was a large scar across his left cheek. Even though he looked exhausted, at least he was alive.

"Is it over?" the shorter of the men asked.

"If it wasn't, I wouldn't be here," Korrev snapped as he unlocked the cage. "Let's go home, Pet."

Korrev wrapped his long, red cape around her nude body and led her back to their bedroom. Some of the palace had been destroyed, but most of it could be easily fixed.

"How was it?" Karin asked softly, because she didn't know what else she should ask after a war had occurred.

"We won." Korrev actually sounded excited. "It was much easier than I anticipated. I was almost bored." He paused. "Your friend Alice got hurt."

Karin stopped in her tracks and shrieked. "What? How? Why didn't you tell me?"

He rolled his eyes. "Because I knew you would get hysterical." He led her into the bedroom. "Besides, she shouldn't have been there in the first place. She disobeyed orders. She's lucky her stupid head wasn't blown off."

"How did she get hurt?" It was a bit hurtful Kyvan had not put Alice in a cage, but Korrev had put her in one.

"She was trying to save Kyvan. She managed to do so, which is quite an impressive feat for such a small human." He started to remove his armor. "She will be all right, Pet. Don't fret. Azis managed to stitch her up. She'll need bed rest for a few weeks, but her mate will make sure she receives it."

Karin was about to scold him for putting her in a cage while the rest of the mates managed to roam free, when she saw Kyvan's bare chest. She gasped.

Korrev frowned. "What is it now?"

There were several deep scars all across his torso, some deeper than others. There were also a few bruises scattered across his collarbone and neck where his armor hadn't been able to offer protection.

"You're hurt." Her voice sounded vulnerable and her body was shaking as it always did when she was about to burst into tears. It was embarrassing. "You should have gone to get checked by Azis first. You could get an infection and get sick—"

"Are you worried about me, little one?" Korrev tilted his head, looking almost amused.

"No!" she snapped. "I just don't want to take care of you if you get sick, just because you were too stubborn to go to a healer."

Korrev approached her and patted her cheek, in an effort to calm her down. She blushed. Since when did she get so emotional? "My wounds are superficial, Pet," he murmured. "Azis had other warriors with more severe injuries, including your little friend. But it is touching you care for me." He played with the pink bow around her neck, reminding her of her pet stature.

She pulled away.

Korrev shook his head. "Let's take a bath and go to bed. You've had too much excitement for one day. It's not good for you."

Karin hesitated. "Do you mean your bed, or my bed?"

"My bed, Pet." Korrev stated as if it should have been obvious. "You'll go back to your bed tomorrow." He pressed her hand against his rock-hard member. How could he be hard after fighting? "Now come, it's time for a bath."

The next morning, Karin was sore all over, from her breasts to between her legs. It seemed war had made Korrev hornier than usual. Despite his injuries, he had managed to fuck her and spank her—playfully this time—until she had to beg him to stop because she was so tired and she didn't have his stamina. It was a good soreness, however, not the terrible type she usually felt after a punishment session.

Both of them must have been tired, because Karin and Korrev slept until noon the next day. Some of his injuries had healed thanks to the healing abilities Krotev aliens had by blood, so his body didn't look as ghastly as it had yesterday.

This gave her some relief, and to think she had been planning his demise earlier.

"Why so sad, Pet?" Korrev asked as he fed her while she was perched on his lap.

"I want to see Alice. I want to make sure she's okay."

"She's okay. I told you she was." Korrev nibbled on her ear in a slight, scolding way.

"I just want to see her. She's my friend."

He sighed. "I will ask Kyvan. She is his mate. If he says no, I will not go against his word. She might be enduring punishment for her foolishness."

"You are the king."

"I will not go against another warrior's rules for his mate, just like they would not dare to tell me how to treat my pet."

His words felt like a slap to the face, even though he had addressed her as a pet before. It just served as a bitter reminder that all the women on this planet were referred to as mates and she was still simply "Pet."

Thankfully, Kyvan allowed Alice and Karin to visit for thirty minutes that evening after dinner. Alice's entire torso was covered in bandages, which caused her to wince every time she moved, and her face was bruised. Other than that, she looked perfectly all right.

"You were a fool," Karin couldn't help but say. Alice was only twenty-two, so she reminded her of a little sister in a way. "You should have never gone into battle."

Alice had the audacity to look amused. "Believe me, Kyvan has told me the same thing constantly. I'm sure my bottom will pay for my foolishness eventually, but I do not want to talk about that." She cocked her head to the side. Alice might be young, but she could read people easily. "Is something wrong, Karin? You seem stressed. Did you see any part of the war? Were you terrified? It was dreadful."

"I didn't see anything," she grumpily responded. "I was in a cage during the entire ordeal."

Alice let out a nervous laugh, not sure how to respond. The fact Karin was a pet and she was a mate had always made her uncomfortable.

Karin looked over her shoulder and saw the men were still talking among themselves in grave tones. The last thing she wanted was to be overheard, but this was important. Especially since she knew Kyvan wouldn't let Alice out of his sight for the next few weeks.

"You're thinking about running away, aren't you?" Alice gave her an understanding smile.

"I am."

"Are you still as unhappy as you were when we first met?"

Karin didn't quite have an answer for that. She wanted to say yes, but it wouldn't be completely true.

She still disliked being punished, of course, and hated not having free will, but the king hadn't been as cruel as he had been during the beginning. Korrev still punished her when he thought she had misbehaved, but he was also protective of her. They would cuddle at night and he would make sure she was served the finest of foods. But she was still just a pet. She would never be a wife, or even a mate.

Karin didn't think she would be happy being a pet for the rest of her life. She needed to return to Earth, even if she would be equally unhappy there for a different reason. At least, on Earth, she had a career. She had a purpose beyond being a breeding mare. She would find a way to be happy without Korrev breathing down her neck.

"Karin?"

"I..." What was she supposed to tell Alice? She was so young, she would never truly understand how complicated her mind was. But it wasn't as complicated as she'd like to think.

She was starting to fall in love with King Korrev. The thought terrified her. Karin had never fallen in love. Not truly anyway, even when she had been dating her long-term boyfriend. But with Korrev, things felt different. She remembered how terrified she had been when she had thought he'd perished during the war.

"Karin." Korrev's sharp tone brought her back to reality. "We must go. Kyvan wants Alice to rest."

"Of course. Goodbye, Alice. Feel better."

He led her away, while he wrapped his arm around her. "What were you two discussing?" He didn't sound accusatory. More like curious.

"Alice thinks she might be pregnant," Karin lied instead. "She doesn't know yet. She'll have to check with Azis. Please keep it a secret from Kyvan until she knows for sure."

"A baby," Korrev mused. "Good. It was time for Kyvan to produce an heir."

Ten

Four months. It had been four months since the battle, and Karin still remained as the king's pet—glued to his side, following him around, sometimes with a leash in hand, warming his bed at night.

Karin couldn't quite come up with an answer as to why she hadn't left already. At first, she thought she was simple cowardly, but then she tried to convince herself she just hadn't found the right time to leave. That part was true, though. Ever since the last battle, Korrev had been more protective than usual. Perhaps because the battle had made Karin even more skittish than usual.

She had only seen Alice in passing since then, as Kyvan didn't want her to leave his quarters until she was fully healed. They had managed to have one more playdate, though. She had begged her to go with her, but Alice had refused. She was happy where she was and she had no desire to leave. Karin couldn't help but envy her happiness. Alice felt secure with Kyvan and Kyvan adored her. She wished she was as lucky as her friend was.

Meanwhile, Karin still felt like she was playing a cat and mouse game with Korrev. She was tired of playing. She did not want to be a pet when there was so much else she could do with her life. Being bred did not excite her, either, like it did Alice. Perhaps she was losing her nerve.

Karin had been known as a firecracker in the courthouse, always winning case after case, but after she came to Krotev, she became more docile. It was like Korrev had spanked the stubbornness out of her. She would be lying if she said she was unhappy. At least not as unhappy as she had been at the very beginning.

"I have a meeting I need to go to." Korrev pressed his lips against her forehead. He had been kissing her more often. Sometimes on the lips, other times on the forehead or against her neck, trying to cover her with hickies.

Korrev didn't drag her to meetings as often as he used to. He trusted her more now.

Karin usually stayed behind and played with her puzzles or read old books some of the other warriors had gotten for their mates and they had discarded.

"Okay."

Korrev frowned, looking concerned. "What's wrong?"

"Nothing," she replied moodily, feeling bratty.

He pressed a hand against her forehead. "Are you coming down with something? It is getting colder."

"No. I'm just tired."

Korrev didn't seem convinced. "I'll have Azis do a checkup on you tomorrow if you're still not feeling better. I can't have you getting sick."

She nodded, only because she knew his patience only went so far. After he left, Karin went towards a small, forgotten chest of drawers near her pet bed. Korrev never checked there so she used it to hide the precious thing she had gotten a mere two weeks ago.

It was a simple gray and white uniform, along with a large matching gray helmet. The one Korrev's pilots used before they flew out in the small spaceships whenever they had to complete orders for the king.

Karin had gotten it when it had fallen from one of the servant's laundry carts. She had kept it ever since. If Korrev ever found it, she would blame it on one of the servants. It was the perfect escape plan.

She would get on one of Korrev's spaceships and just return to Earth. It surely wouldn't be hard, would it? They were more advanced after all.

Karin closed her eyes. It was now or never. She might never have another opportunity to escape again. She had to do this now, before it became colder and Korrev would spend more time inside, or before she became pregnant.

Before she chickened out, she put on the uniform. It was baggy on her, but it did a good job of hiding her curves. The helmet was a bit heavy, but she would just have to bear it.

The only problem was the bow around her neck. She had to get it off. It was the only thing holding her back. It contained a chip. If she didn't remove it, the king would easily find her again. She needed to find the key which opened it. Korrev usually removed the bow at bathtimes, but he had never shown her where he hid the key.

Karin started ransacking the bedroom, pulling open drawers and overturning clothes in every direction. After thirty minutes of endless searching, she finally found it hidden inside one of his armors which was so heavy, she could barely lift it. It was a small golden key. To think this little key held her freedom.

"Please fit," she begged silently as she jammed the key in the keyhole below the large pink bow. A sigh of relief escaped from her the second she heard the small clicking sound. The bow fell off easily, and she rubbed her neck.

Finally.

There was no going back now. She put on the helmet, and

without a look back, she headed towards the back of the palace where she knew the ships deployed from.

No one questioned her, but they gave her odd looks because she was walking around with her helmet.

Karin's heart was thumping loudly inside her chest when she finally made it to the platform where the ships descended from.

"You're late, 84." A grouchy-looking alien, wearing a similar uniform, looked up from the screen in front of him. "Your ship is number four. Do you have the documents the king wants you to deliver?"

Karin nodded, touching the big pocket on the side of the uniform, hoping she wasn't questioned.

He didn't. "Good. Off you go, 84. See you when you return."

Karin nodded, shuffling towards the ship. It was bigger than she had anticipated, even though it was sort of square-shaped and could only fit one person.

She got into the ship awkwardly and closed the door. She couldn't believe she was actually doing this. In reality, she only wanted to run in the opposite direction and jump into Korrev's arms.

"You can do this, Karin." She bit her lower lip. "Don't be a baby."

The dashboard in front of her had at least thirty buttons of different colors and sizes. This only made her more nervous.

"84!" the alien who greeted her barked at her over the intercom. "Why haven't you left yet? Is there something wrong with the ship?"

"No!" she managed to squeak, not caring that her voice sounded feminine. She pulled on the lever in front of her and started pushing as many buttons as she could. Hopefully, it did something. She really didn't want to get caught.

The ship roared to life and dashed out of the platform so fast, she was surprised she didn't end up vomiting on herself.

Karin's heart dropped when she realized she was no longer

on Krotev. She was in space, and it was marvelous. She didn't know how else to describe it. Everything was so dark and vast and out of the ordinary. Who knew space could be so wonderful?

She frowned. She wondered if she would be able to properly breathe without this helmet, which seemed to be providing her with oxygen. She was fine in Krotev, but she wasn't sure if it was safe to take it off.

Karin would have nothing to worry about if she managed to reach Earth. But as she looked at the row of buttons on the screen, she was starting to think it might be impossible. She just wanted to go home.

Home. Was she really starting to think of Krotev as home? She hadn't even been there a year! Karin was starting to think she hadn't really thought this through.

Then she thought about Korrev and how she would no longer see him after today. She thought about his blond hair, his icy blue eyes, and his smirk. For some reason, it made her feel sad.

She rode on the ship for what felt like hours. Eventually, her stomach started growling and she made the discovery that she had stupidly forgotten to pack food in her hurry. She didn't have food and she desperately needed to pee.

Karin looked at the screen in front of her. It was a map, but she didn't know how to read it. She had never seen anything so complicated. She wasn't even sure if she was heading in the right direction towards Earth.

Karin Johansson had graduated from a top university and had gone to law school. She always thought things through. Today, might have been the exception.

She couldn't help but wonder if Korrev would come searching for her. It would be straight out of a romance film, though she guessed Korrev would be more furious. But how was he even supposed to track her down if she didn't have her collar?

Karin concluded she had spent too much time in Krotev. It was the reason her brain had turned to mush. She didn't do anything but sleep, eat, and fuck Korrev.

Her thoughts were drifting once again to Korrev, when the ship started making a loud, wailing noise.

"Stop it!" she whined as she pushed several buttons, hoping it would do something, but the wailing just continued. There was a nearby planet right in front of her. It wasn't Earth, but it would have to do until she got the stupid ship fixed. Karin pulled the lever and closed her eyes. If she died landing this thing, she hoped it would be a quick death.

The air left her body as the ship landed rapidly. It was a miracle nothing had broken. Karin allowed herself a few minutes for her heart to settle down. Then she gingerly opened the door and stepped outside.

This planet was vast and empty, unlike Krotev which was an empire. The land was green and there were a few plantlike objects like the trees she had seen back in Krotev. But that was it. No people. No aliens. No buildings. No life whatsoever. She didn't know if it was a good or a bad thing.

Karin gingerly took off her helmet. She didn't know if this planet had oxygen. She hoped it did. She didn't want to wear this helmet around, not to mention she didn't know how much oxygen she had left.

Her body relaxed when she realized she could breathe properly without the helmet.

"Hello!" she called out. "Hello!"

No response.

Karin looked wearily at the ship, which she wasn't sure even worked anymore. Then she burst into tears. She desperately wanted to go home.

〜

Korrev was not someone who lacked confidence. In fact, people had often said he was much too arrogant. However, he didn't mind them. When one was king, he had to be arrogant and confident, or his throne might disappear.

He couldn't help but smile as he looked down at his palm. He was carrying a small box of chocolates which was a true delicacy in Krotev. The men didn't like them. They were too sweet for them, but the human women adored them, which was why the king ordered his warriors to go purchase them whenever they were rounding up new mates.

Korrev could have brought forth their entire supply of chocolate from the kitchen, but he was sure Karin would finish it in one afternoon. He didn't want to spoil her even if she had been rather good lately. He felt like he could trust her more and he was no longer afraid of leaving her alone. She had even become more docile and adorable. Hence, the gift of chocolate. She could be a sweetheart when she wanted to be. Perhaps it wouldn't be bad if he spoiled her every once in a while.

"Karin." Korrev entered the bedroom, but he saw no one. Karin was not in her usual lounging spot by the window. A chill ran down his spine when he didn't see his pet. "Karin! Come out now! I order you to!"

Silence.

Korrev refused to let panic settle in, but it was hard not to. He checked the bath, the rest of the bedroom, and the dining area, but still no trace of Karin. He felt something beneath his boot.

Karin's pink bow. The little brat had managed to take it off, so he had no way of contacting her.

The panic he was feeling started to grow, despite his best efforts to control it. Karin was gone. She could be anywhere in the palace, or worse, outside. Without her bow, he would have no way of tracking her down.

Damn her. Damn her! He should have never trusted her!

"Bozan!" he roared.

His main servant, a young man who had barely reached adulthood, entered the bedroom looking panicked. His panic grew when he saw the king's angry face. "Yes, Your Majesty?"

"Where is she?"

"Where's who?"

"Karin!"

"Your pet?"

Korrev wanted to pummel the fool for being so stupid, but it wasn't his fault Karin had disappeared. It was his own. He should have never trusted her fully. He was the stupid one.

"Order all of the warriors in the palace to search for Karin. Tell them they must check every room."

"Yes, Your Majesty."

It took twenty minutes for his warriors to tell him there was no trace of Karin inside the palace. It took them another fifteen minutes to realize she had somehow managed to escape on a ship. A ship they couldn't track.

If he hadn't been so angry, Korrev would have been impressed by her determination to get away from him.

After giving his warriors orders to track down whatever information they could gather about the missing ship, Korrev started mentally thinking about the nearby planets. There weren't many, but they were certainly less friendly than Krotev.

Someone placed a hand on his shoulder.

Kyvan.

He looked concerned and he hated the look of pity on his face. He *hated* that look.

"I heard what happened with Karin. Is there anything I can do?"

"No!" Korrev snarled back. "Does Alice know about Karin's escape? Did they plan this together?"

"Of course not!" Kyvan looked offended, almost angry. "My

little Alice is safe in my quarters. She has hardly spoken to Karin. She's been too busy focusing on healing her injuries."

"Well, someone had to have planned this." Korrev kicked a chair over angrily. "Someone must have convinced Karin to do this. *To leave me.*"

Kyvan hesitated a bit before he spoke. "You forget that Karin was deeply unhappy. She was not even your mate; she was your pet, an even lower position. You punished her cruelly even though I warned you against it. How does it surprise you that she left?"

Korrev gave him a cold smile. "I will still be speaking to Alice on this matter. I'm sure she has something to say."

"You will not!" Kyvan snarled back. "She is resting and she has just announced she's with child. You will not disturb her, Korrev."

Korrev raised his eyebrow and simply said, "I am king." Then he headed to Kyvan's quarters to speak to Alice. If he found out Alice had a hand in this, he would consider it betrayal.

He was a king very few people would cross.

Eleven

Karin didn't know how long she had been stranded. She had stopped counting the days weeks ago, but she knew it had been more than two months on this unnamed planet. She had bitterly regretted leaving ever since.

There was no one here. Hadn't been since she had first arrived. She didn't know if it was a blessing or a curse. She only knew she would rather get punished every day than be here for one more second.

She would get on her hands and knees and beg for forgiveness to Korrev if only he would take her back. Karin would swallow her pride and be his pet and the mother of his children if he would only take her back to Krotev.

Karin couldn't help but let out a bitter laugh. She had spent all this time trying to gain her freedom back, and when she had, she was miserable. But in her defense, she had wanted to return to Earth, not this unknown planet.

Karin had found an emergency supply kit on the back of the ship when it was clear the stupid thing wouldn't fly again. For weeks, she had tried to communicate with someone back in

Krotev by pushing every button she could find, but with little luck.

The emergency supply kit had held four gallons of water and a ton of food since Krotev aliens usually needed a lot of food to survive. She hadn't been worried at first about her food/water ration, but she was worried now.

She only allowed herself half a glass of water a day and very little food, in order to make sure the food lasted as long as possible. But every day, she saw her supplies dwindling, which made her nervous. If she didn't find extra food or water fast, she was going to die a very painful death.

Once or twice, the thought of ending it all had crossed Karin's mind, but she was too afraid to do so. Instead, she decided to try her best to survive.

She was still wearing the uniform she had stolen as she did not have any other clothes, but it was dirty and unkempt. Not to mention, she desperately needed a bath. She felt very dirty and her hair desperately needed shampooing. But there was no way she would waste her precious water source to clean herself.

Karin woke up one day feeling very tired. It seemed she was tired often because she didn't get the proper nutrients. Often, she felt like the only thing she did was sleep. Sleep was her escape. It was the only time she felt decently happy, because in those dreams, she was often on Earth, treating herself to an after-work drink, or back on Krotev, sleeping in Korrev's arms while he called her his pet.

"Food, Karin," she mumbled to herself as she walked away from the spaceship to continue exploring. "Find food first, and then you need to find water."

She was trying to remain hopeful, but it was terribly hard. She didn't have much energy left, her lips were chapped, her body dirty, and her stomach hurt all the time because she was always hungry.

There were a couple of trees on this planet, but nothing that grew any type of the strange fruit she had seen on Krotev. Sometimes if she was feeling desperate enough, Karin would swallow some of the leaves or put some in her half cup of water in a weak attempt to make tea.

This time, she would have to walk even farther if she wanted to find food or water. But this planet was dry. It wasn't surprising no one had bothered living on it for years.

She walked until she felt her feet were swelling from so much exercising. She allowed herself a sip of water, but no more.

Karin stiffened when she saw a bush a few feet away, filled with bright orange berries. She used the last of her energy to race towards them. It almost seemed too good to be true. She took one of the berries and inspected it.

It was small, round, and plump, a bright orange color which reminded her of oranges. She would kill for orange juice right about now. Karin had no way of knowing if they were safe to eat, but she was so hungry, she would eat wood right about now. She placed two berries in her mouth and ate them hungrily. They were delicious. They kind of tasted like candy. Karin doubted she had ever tasted anything so glorious. She ate two. Then four. Then six, until she felt her belly was full and satisfied.

Then Karin started to feel sleepy. Her miraculous discovery earned her a well-deserved nap. She managed to make a soft little bed in the bushes. After she woke up, she would search for water. Maybe her luck was changing.

Karin closed her eyes. She began to dream.

Karin was wrapped in Korrev's strong, protective arms. It was one of the rare occasions when he allowed her to sleep with him and not on her pet bed. She liked sleeping with him. Not that she would ever admit it, of course. Her pride wouldn't let her.

But she did enjoy sleeping in his arms and having him kiss her forehead. For a few delicious moments, she felt like his equal instead of a pet.

"What shall we do today, Karin?" he asked her as he entwined his hand in hers.

"I want to explore Krotev," she whispered as she snuggled closer to him. "I feel like I've hardly seen any of it. Alice has."

"That's because Alice behaves. Kyvan also has a bad habit of spoiling her." Korrev smirked at her. "But if you wish, Pet, I will take you to explore. Would you like that?"

Karin smiled as she snuggled closer to him. "I would love it very much."

"Karin!" Korrev's voice suddenly changed. It sounded worried. Angry. Then everything became dark.

Twelve

Korrev had found her. It had taken four months and six days and an endless number of hours, but he had finally found her.

He had driven his warriors mad, as well as the men who took care of the technology in the palace. Korrev had sent more men than he could think of to different planets, some which took days or weeks to reach.

Korrev wasn't an idiot. He knew his men harbored resentment, but he didn't care. All he cared about was having Karin back in his arms. If he had to search under every rock, so be it.

Kyvan had told him multiple times to forget about the blonde, especially since they were getting multiple shipments of human females every few weeks. The last time he had brought up forgetting Karin, he and Kyvan had gotten into a physical altercation. It had taken six guards to pull them apart because Korrev had been blinded by rage,

"The girl is messing with your head," Kyvan finally said with a bloody lip. "Either get her back, or forget about her, because you're not acting like a king ought to act. Your head is all over the place."

So that's what Korrev did. He searched every planet he could.

He even asked for favors from people he didn't particularly like, but it had to be done. He was going in blind. Karin didn't have her tracker and she had destroyed the one on the ship.

He had even sent Kyvan back to Earth, to New York City specifically, to see if she had returned. This had made Kyvan unhappy because he had to be away from a very pregnant Alice. He had done so, anyway, because it was the king's wish.

Kyvan had reported back that her apartment had been vacated due to a lack of payment and he had used his human form to inquire about her at her old place of employment. But no one had seen her. It seemed she had not returned to Earth. He didn't know if it was a good thing or a bad thing.

Kyvan was growing increasingly frustrated as time went on, and it seemed he was lashing out at everyone. He had always been proud of his ability to maintain a cool head, but Karin had taken it away from him.

They had searched every planet nearby, and unfortunately, there was no news of Karin. He didn't think any of the leaders of those planets had her. They would surely fear his wrath if they had her. The ship she had taken had been one of the smaller ones, so she couldn't have gotten far.

One of his men had finally pointed out that they hadn't searched the vacant planets nearby. Korrev felt stupid they hadn't checked them, but then again, he'd never thought Karin would go to an empty planet by choice. Had something gone wrong with the ship? She wasn't always the most coordinated.

They checked some of the smaller planets first, and when they had become unsuccessful, they checked the larger ones. This was the last planet they needed to check near Krotev. Korrev grew uneasy in his seat as the ship landed on the dusty planet. The planet was simply known as Gativ. No one had bothered to inhabit it because it was a dusty, uninteresting planet. Nothing could grow there. The weather was usually warm and it was farther from the other planets. As a result, very few people visited it and usually for less than an hour.

"We're here, Your Majesty."

Korrev, along with the other warriors, exited the ship. He tried not to get too excited. Karin hadn't been on the other planets. Why on earth would she be on this one?

After splitting the warriors into three different teams, for a faster search, Korrev made his way towards where his group was supposed to go. He, along with the others, were in their gray alien form, not in the human one. They were faster in this form and their senses heightened.

After twenty minutes of walking, he stopped short. *Her scent.* He recognized it. It was Karin's scent. He would be able to recognize it anywhere.

"Karin!" Korrev roared, hardly recognizing his own voice. It was a mix of terror and hope, with a bit of desperation.

Korrev could hardly believe his luck. Karin was here. After four long months, he had finally found his pet. And this time, he would never let her go. Even if he had to chain himself to her every day.

The king followed her scent, leaving the others behind. They were moving too slowly. He finally found her huddled in one of the bushes like a small animal. She was wearing the same pilot uniform she had stolen four months ago. It was dirty and she desperately needed a bath.

He didn't care. The only thing he could think about was how much he wanted to kiss her and then fuck her into submission.

"Karin!" he roared. If the little brat was pretending to be asleep as a way to plead for mercy, he was going to be pissed. She was already in a boatload of trouble.

But Karin didn't stir, even as he was practically screaming in her ear. It was like she couldn't hear him.

Korrev's annoyance diminished as he gave her shoulder a little shove. "Karin?"

Dread filled his body when he realized Karin was not simply asleep. He checked her pulse and found her heart was still beating, but very slowly. She was pale. Malnourished. Sickly.

Something had happened before he managed to get to her. He didn't think starvation was the culprit, though it was a possibility. There seemed to be something else entirely wrong with her.

Korrev picked her up in his arms. He hated how frail she felt in his arms, like a limp doll. He kept calling her by her name, hoping she would answer, but she didn't.

Jix, one of his warriors, called out to him, "Your Majesty—"

Korrev froze when he looked at the bright orange berries more closely. He wasn't a healer and wasn't particularly interested in healing, especially when he had other people to do the job for him. His father thought differently. He'd told him it was important that, as future king, he was schooled in various subjects.

Korrev needed to get her to a healer. He needed to get her out of this hellish planet and towards home, a place where he could keep her warm and safe. Where he could protect her from anything that went wrong.

However, he had remembered one of the lessons Azis had given him regarding poisons. One of the lessons has been on small, orange berries which grew in clusters in bushes. Korrev had all of them burned to the ground when he became king so no one accidentally ate them and became poisoned. But it didn't mean the poisonous berries didn't grow on other planets.

Karin must have swallowed them in her desperation to get some food in her belly. He remembered Azis saying it was a slow acting poison. There was a very good chance Karin might be saved.

"Get Azis on the telecommunicator. Now!" Korrev said

through gritted teeth when Jix continued giving him a stupid look. How could he have been stupid enough to not bring a healer along with them? But he had never thought his precious Karin would be hurt. He had thought she had landed on a planet where she would have food and shelter even if she was a captive. How foolish he had been.

Neither he nor his men knew anything about healing. They could remove weapons from the body, fix limbs temporarily, and stop the bleeding. But neither he nor his men knew anything about poison. It was not something they often dealt with, and even if they did, they always had the grumpy Azis or one of the healers to take over.

Jix finally bowed to him. "Yes, Your Majesty. What about the others?"

Korrev fought the urge to slap him. Didn't he see how important this was? "We will come back for the others. We need to return to Krotev *now*. Let Azis know we are on our way and he had better be ready for us."

The trip back to Krotev was short, only about forty-five minutes. Yet, for the king, it felt like the longest moments of his life. He used the time to stroke Karin's blonde hair from her sweaty forehead. Her fever was getting higher as the minutes passed by and she was growing paler, even though her cheeks were rosy from how feverish she was.

He whispered sweet nothings into her ear, something he had never done with anyone else, which caused his warriors to exchange odd looks. Korrev didn't care what they thought or said. His only concern was that his pet was comfortable.

"Ko," she mumbled in her sleep, but it was the extent of her words. She didn't say much after that and he didn't pressure her. She needed all the rest she could possibly get. She was talking. She was breathing. For Korrev, it was enough.

Azis was waiting for them once the ship landed. He barely blinked when Korrev exited the ship, still carrying Karin.

"One of your warriors said she consumed something," Azis said plainly as Korrev practically ran to the infirmary. "What was it?"

"Berries. Those little orange ones. The ones that grow on bushes. You said they were slow acting poison." They finally made it to the infirmary and he placed her on the bed. He took a dagger and ripped open her clothes.

Both men grimaced when they saw her ribs poking out and how malnourished she was.

"She needs a bath."

"A bath is the least of her concerns." Azis went to his cabinets and started opening them. He pulled out several bottles filled with different colored liquid, along with his medical tools. "I need to act fast if I want to save your pet. It's a miracle she's not dead yet. Most humans would have perished the minute they took their first bite."

Korrev gripped his arm. "You said it was a slow acting poison!"

"It is." Azis pulled away and started drawing some blood from Karin to test. "For us. We have a stronger immune system. Humans are delicate, especially human females. You seem to forget, the smallest gust of wind can knock them down. It's a miracle their species has survived as long as they have."

"But she will live, correct?" It took all his willpower not to strangle Azis, even though he knew deep down it wasn't the healer's fault. Karin had to live. She needed to live, for him. For herself. He doubted he would be able to function without his pet by his side.

Azis grimaced as he looked at Korrev wearily, as if afraid of how the young king would react. "I will try my best to save her," he said slowly. "But this type of poison acts fast on humans. It causes the organs to shut down. It's a miracle she has lived as long as she has. If she does not make it, I will make sure, at least, her death is comfortable—"

"You will save her."

"Korrev, be reasonable. There are other human females. Just because she was foolish enough to run off, doesn't mean there won't be others to warm your bed at night."

"You will save her," Korrev repeated again. "You will do everything in your power to do so. I do not want another female. I want *her*. Is it clear?"

He gave a little nod of his head. "Yes, Your Majesty." He hesitated. "You need to leave the room. I and the rest of the healers cannot work while you are prancing around the room like a caged animal."

"I won't leave Karin."

"Then, at least, stand outside of the infirmary and let me work. I will provide hourly updates."

Korrev grudgingly did as he was told. He knew Karin was in the best hands.

Korrev was forced to sit outside the infirmary even if it irritated him to do so. The wait was painfully long, even though he knew Azis was one of the best healers out there. Karin would be fine. She had to be fine; otherwise, he was determined to make everyone else's lives painfully miserable. It still surprised him how much he had come to care for the misbehaving brat. He had never cared for anyone before, with the exception of Kyvan. Yet Karin had wormed her way into his heart, first, with her determination, then later, with her warmness when her guard was done. He closed his eyes, hating how helpless he felt.

If Karin were to die, he didn't know what he would do. It would be a cruel twist of fate if he had worked so hard to get her back, only to lose her at the very last second. Kyvan had been the only one brave enough to ask why he didn't just give up when it became apparent she wouldn't be found so easily.

He had simply said he was not a person who wished to be outsmarted, but it had been a lie. Korrev had simply not wanted to lose her, but he was, of course, not going to confess it to anyone else. Not even Kyvan, even though he would understand better than anyone how he was feeling because he was so enamored with his little Alice.

For months, he had been worried sick that Karin was being mistreated, or worse, but it turned out she had been much closer than he had anticipated. This only just made him even more irritated. He should have checked abandoned planets as well. He was so stupid. Now, Karin could die because of his own foolishness.

No, he refused to accept the fact. So what if she had poisoned herself? He had gotten there in time and Azis was a genius. She would live. She had to live.

"Are you well? You look irritated."

Korrev had been so distracted, he hadn't even heard his best friend come in. To be honest, he had been avoiding Kyvan lately. Alice was heavily pregnant and due to give birth any day now.

He had been so miserable lately that being in the same room as Kyvan, who was so annoyingly happy, would only cause his misery to grow, and it wasn't like he could ask his best friend to be unhappy. It was his first child so, of course, he should be happy.

"Azis is working on Karin," he told his friend. Kyvan pursed his lips. "She might not make it."

"I heard she ate the poisonous orange berries." He clicked his tongue in sympathy. "Do not concern yourself too much. He is an excellent healer. If anyone can nurse her back to health, it is Azis."

"You forget she is human," the king said. "Their immune system is not as strong as ours. There is a good chance she will die. I wouldn't get my hopes up."

Kyvan didn't say anything. How could he, when he was just as practical a person as he was. "How's Alice?" Korrev asked instead.

Kyvan brightened at the question like Korrev knew he

would. "She is in excellent health. Though Azis worries the baby might be too big. He has her on a diet, to prevent her from gaining too much weight, but you know Alice can't say no to sweets."

He let Kyvan talk for the next thirty minutes about the baby, the nursery, and how adorable Alice was. Korrev wasn't interested, if he was being completely honest, but he was glad his friend was happy. At least, he was distracted from Karin's illness.

"She'll be all right, Korrev. If she has managed to survive living with you for almost a year, she can survive anything," Kyvan joked.

"I have been pretty terrible to her, haven't I?" Korrev grimaced. "I wanted to break her and I did, but as a result, she tried to leave me forever. She almost died because of my own selfishness."

Kyvan didn't say anything. There was nothing he could say. Korrev was right. She had left because of him.

Kyvan rapidly changed the topic and he managed to distract the king long enough that he didn't fret about Karin.

Close to midnight, Azis returned to find them. He looked exhausted but not unhappy, which meant Karin had lived.

"Is she alive?" Korrev demanded.

"She is." Azis looked weary. "But barely. I managed to prevent her organs from shutting down completely, but I still had to give her several blood transfusions and several medications." He hesitated. "But, Your Majesty, I do not want you to get your hopes up. Your pet is still very, very sick."

"She's alive," was all he said. "That's all that matters. If she survived so far, then she has a chance. Thank you." Azis looked surprised at his thankfulness. "May I see her?"

"Only for a few minutes. She's very tired."

"I want you to be her primary healer. Around the clock care. The other healers can take care of everyone else."

"Of course."

Kyvan gave him a pat on the back before he departed. The king practically burst into the room.

He saw Karin on one of the beds at the end of the room. She was covered in heavy blankets. Although her face still looked flushed, it was apparent her fever was down. The paleness of her skin still concerned him, but at least she wasn't near death this time.

"Hi, Pet," he murmured as he sat down in a hard chair next to her. "Wake up for me, Pet. Please. It's an order."

Karin didn't stir. It was like she hadn't even heard him. He hated seeing her like this, so unmoving, so still. It made him worry Azis was right and he shouldn't get his hopes up.

"Karin, Pet. Can you hear me?"

Nothing.

He sighed. "You must be a very strong, brave pet and wake up for me. You had me worried sick for months. You cannot keep worrying me."

But she didn't wake up. She only made slight, wheezing noises which worried him very much. Azis had mentioned something earlier about the berries possibly messing up her lungs.

Hopefully, it would be fixed; otherwise, she would breathe like a broken machine for the rest of her life, and neither of them would like that.

Every bone in his body ached and he realized he hadn't slept in over twenty-four hours, possibly more if he was being honest. He'd only been getting a wink of sleep in the months following her disappearance. But he should sleep, especially since she wouldn't become well again in the blink of an eye.

Korrev leaned over and kissed her on her dry lips. "Sleep, Pet," he murmured as he pushed her blonde hair away from her face. "I will see you in the morning."

The days slowly passed. Korrev was losing his patience. Azis had warned him Karin's recovery would take weeks, possibly months, but he hadn't expected the wait to be so terribly long.

Karin still hadn't woken up, but some of the color had returned to her cheeks. The wheezing in her lungs wasn't as loud as it once was, but to be honest, he hadn't been pleased by her progress.

"What is taking so long?" He scowled at Azis one afternoon. "She should be awake by now."

"She's making the necessary progress," Azis informed him. "You can't expect her to wake up and pretend nothing is wrong. She's human, in case you have forgotten, Your Majesty. The fact she is alive is miraculous in itself."

He scowled.

Azis had known him since he was a boy, and therefore, the only one brave enough besides Kyvan to speak to him like that. He also knew he would never kill him. Azis was much too talented to lose.

"You can't breed her yet, not for several months if that's what you are concerned about," Azis suddenly blurted out.

"What?" he snapped.

"You can't impregnate her until I clear her," Azis repeated again. "If you want someone to carry your baby, might I suggest you look for someone else?"

"I am not thinking about impregnating anyone." Korrev sounded almost offended. "All I care is Karin being well again and not stuck in a bed for the rest of her life. Having a baby, is the least of my concerns."

Azis nodded as he patted him on his shoulder. "She will wake up. The mere fact she survived the poison and is healing is a miracle in itself."

Korrev tried not to lose hope, but he felt like he was fighting a losing battle.

Three days after his conversation with Azis, Korrev found himself ditching all of the meetings he was required to go to, choosing instead to sit by Karin's bedside.

It had been two weeks since they had rescued her. She looked almost healthy. As if she were simply sleeping and not recovering from the poisoning.

"Karin," he murmured as he stroked the inside of her wrist. "How much longer are you going to torture me? Please wake up for me, Pet."

Silence.

He didn't know what else to say. He wasn't very expressive, and to be honest, he was willing to promise her anything she wanted as long as she woke up. Jewels, gold, a bigger room, anything which would please her. But he knew deep down there would only be one thing which would make her happy.

Her freedom.

"I'll give it to you," his voice cracked, even though it was obvious she couldn't hear him. "I'll give you the freedom you so desire. I'll let you return to Earth. Just please wake up."

A little moan escaped her lips, so unexpectedly, he nearly jumped back in response.

Was she waking up?

It sounded too good to be true.

"Karin?" he tried again. "Pet, open your eyes for me. Please." He rarely said the word please. It sounded strange coming from him, but he would beg on his hands and knees if it meant Karin would talk to him again.

Another little moan. This time, a bit louder.

He rubbed the inside of her wrist, as if trying to soothe her awake. "Pet, Pet, you have made me wait too long. Wake up for me. Now."

It was as if her body had heard the command. Her blue eyes shot open, her mouth widened as if gasping for breath.

She looked around the room, obviously perplexed. She almost looked adorable. "Korrev."

The name sounded lovely on her lips. He had been waiting for her to say something. Anything. And she had said his name.

"It's me, sweetheart." He pressed his palm against her face, cupping her chin, trying to look at her.

Karin squirmed, obviously believing she was in trouble.

Her blue eyes kept looking around, quickly recognizing the infirmary. "I'm back on Krotev." Her voice was calm. Not happy, but not exactly disappointed, either.

"You are."

"You rescued me?"

"Who else would have? You broke my ship the minute you left."

A strange smile wobbled on her lips. "You need a better ship."

"And you need to stop acting without thinking." He didn't immediately address the question he wanted to ask her. "You got sick. When we picked you up, you were nearly dead."

"Sick from what?"

"The orange berries you ate were poisonous. Fatal to humans. Quite honestly, it's a miracle you are even alive."

She nodded silently. "You saved me?"

"Barely."

"How did you find me? I didn't have my collar on."

"I have my ways. Which reminds me that after you are better, I am going to sew the new collar against your throat. Maybe that way, you won't take it off."

Her blue eyes widened, unsure if he was joking or not.

Korrev decided to change the conversation. The last thing he needed was to have her burst into tears. Azis would not be pleased with him if she started crying in her condition.

"How are you feeling?"

"Tired," Karin admitted. There were dark circles underneath her eyes. Even her lips looked lifeless. "Every bone in my body aches, and my lungs feel heavy. I'm struggling to breathe. It feels like I just ran a marathon."

"Azis struggled to remove the poison from your body. It was

affecting your lungs and the rest of your organs. He had to give you a blood transfusion. You will likely feel pretty sickly for the next few weeks. There will be plenty of bed rest and plenty of tonics."

She nodded, looking too miserable to argue.

"Are you hungry, Pet?"

"No."

"Too bad. I'm sending the servants out for food and you will eat some of it, Karin, even if I have to sit you on my lap and force feed you myself."

Karin pouted but didn't argue. To be fair, she still looked very disoriented.

A servant brought the food. When Korrev noticed she picked at it, he gave an exhausted little sigh and spoon fed her himself some porridge-like soup. She only ate half of it and he was satisfied.

After the light dinner, she began to feel sleepy again. It was clear she had a million questions to ask him, but she was too tired to do so.

"Korrev—"

"No," he interrupted as he tucked her into bed. "It can wait until morning."

"But—"

"Karin, don't displease me when you just woke up, unless you want to pick another switch. I'm already cross with you."

She blushed but didn't argue anymore as she cuddled against the four or so blankets he insisted she needed, even though she was plenty warm enough.

"I can't believe I was brought back," she mumbled.

"Is it a good thing, or something which displeases you?" he asked as gently as he could, even though he desperately wanted to know the answer.

But Karin didn't answer him. She was already fast asleep.

Thirteen

The next few days were strange for Karin Johansson. She couldn't remember the last time she'd been fussed over. Not even during the few times she dated.

She had grown up as an orphan after her mother's death, so being fussed over was not something she was used to. In fact, once or twice, Korrev had to scold her and remind her that her only job was to remain in bed even though all she wanted to do was stretch out her limbs after weeks of being forced to lie down.

A few times, she had teased him and called him the best nursemaid ever, something he had answered to with a scowl.

"Don't you have anything else more important to do?" she asked him once. He was driving her and Azis crazy, but neither of them had convinced him to leave for a few hours.

"There's nothing more important than you," he had simply said as he tucked the blanket around her.

At first, Korrev's acts of kindness were strange but adorable. He made sure she ate her meals every day, even if she complained that she was stuffed. He would order the servants to give her the best blankets and anything else to keep her entertained, so she remained in bed. When he wanted her to go to sleep, he would cuddle her and stroke her hair until she fell asleep.

But even though Korrev was acting almost gentlemanly, she couldn't help but be nervous. She had never expected him to find her, and now that he had, she had expected shouting, or at the very least, a whipping, but neither of those things had happened. Instead, he was almost loving with her, as if he was afraid she would break.

Karin looked at him one morning when they were finishing their breakfast.

He raised a pale eyebrow as if daring her to speak.

She wrapped her robe around her body. This was one of those happy occasions when Korrev had finally given her what she wanted, clothes. Even though she had clothes now, she was still feeling terribly cold. She had also lost her curves. Her breasts and hips were basically non-existent. She hadn't been this slim since she was a high school student.

"Karin, if you have something to say, then just say it." He took a sip of his drink. "Staring at me with eyes of wonder will not do anything to make our conversation go further."

She hesitated. "Why haven't you punished me?"

"Do you want to be punished?"

"No!" she blurted out. "But I just feel like I'm waiting for the other shoe to drop."

He looked annoyed, obviously, not understanding the human phrase. "What are you trying to say? Speak plainly."

"I'm just wondering what's next? Do I go back to being your pet?"

"We're not there yet," was all he said. She was still sick, even though the cough in her lungs had gotten better, but she was still sleeping more than normal and wasn't very hungry, either.

"I want to know," she whined.

Korrev glared at her. "Do you want a spanking?"

"No," she mumbled as she looked at her lap. "But I would

like to know things. I don't like being kept in the dark, Korrev. Just tell me what's going to happen after I'm fully healed?"

For a second, he did not speak, which only made her more nervous. Maybe he was planning on dumping her somewhere else because she was so disobedient.

"It's up to you," he simply said.

"What? What does that mean?"

"Did you hear me when you were asleep? Before you awoke completely?"

"Obviously not," she answered tensely.

Korrev almost smiled. "I promised you if you woke up, which you did, I would give you your freedom."

Karin blinked at him, waiting for the punchline, obviously not believing him. Why would this tyrant give her freedom, just like that, after making her life difficult for months? He kept her as his pet, looked for her for months, then suddenly, he would just let her go?

"You seem surprised, Pet. I thought you would be jumping for joy." He didn't sound amused. In fact, he sounded almost a bit sad.

"I just never thought you would give me my freedom. You said I would be your pet always. You're not someone who changes your mind."

"That was before your desperation caused you to be foolish, Karin. You nearly died. I will not have you risking your life because you want to leave." He grimaced. "I would rather let you leave on your own, than be the one responsible for your death."

Karin didn't say anything. She just stared at her lap. This was what she had been wanting all along. Then, why wasn't she happy?

"What's wrong, Pet?" he asked with a wry smile. "Are you having second thoughts?"

"Don't be silly. I've been wanting to leave." Karin couldn't hide the crack in her voice. "How would you do it? Would you just plop me back on Earth?"

"Not exactly. We would have to erase your memories before we do."

Erase her memories? "Why?"

Korrev gave her a wry smile. "We can't have you exposing our secrets to the humans. Not that they would believe you. Believe me, it's quite painless. We'll drop you off on Earth. It would be like waking up after a bad dream."

A bad dream?

If they had asked her at the very beginning of her abduction, she would have described the entire ordeal as a very bad dream. However, now, she wasn't so sure.

She should jump at the chance at being free, but strangely, she was having second thoughts. If her memory was erased, she would forget about her time in Krotev. About Alice, Kyvan, and Azis. She would even forget about Korrev.

She would forget about the blond king who was sometimes sweet and other times harsh. Who would sometimes stroke her hair until she fell asleep. Who would punish her if she was bratty and who would praise her when she behaved well.

The answer was obvious. She should return home to the life she once led. A life where she was a successful lawyer, living in her glamorous penthouse in New York. But then she remembered her life back then. Had she been happy? The answer was no. She had been overworked and spent more time at work than at home. She had also been lonely. Karin couldn't remember the last time she had a friend or been somewhere not work related.

Life in Krotev was far from perfect, but at least she had formed somewhat of a family here. She and Alice were friends. She got along with Kyvan and Azis. And Korrev? Korrev was complicated.

She did not hate him as much as she had when he had first made her his pet. In fact, dare she say she had even grown attached to him? When Karin had been stranded, he had taken over her thoughts. Her desires. To the point that, at night when she had been alone, Korrev had consumed her every thought.

Once or twice, she had admitted to herself she would do anything to see him again. When she had woken up and found him staring at her, she had thought it was a dream, not a nightmare. The first word that had come to her mind had been joy. Joy, because she had been reunited with Korrev.

Now, he was giving her her freedom. Suddenly, she didn't want it.

As if sensing her turmoil, he chuckled. "Are you having second thoughts, Pet? Perhaps you are a glutton for punishment."

Karin didn't laugh. "I wouldn't remember anyone? Not even you?"

"Correct." Korrev gave her a wry smile. "It would be as if you and I had never existed together. That is what you wanted, didn't you?"

She bit on a nail. "No. Not really. I'm not sure. Could I come visit you or Alice?"

"We are not exactly a vacation destination, Karin. Once you decide to leave, you are gone for good. So, what is your answer?"

Karin didn't speak for a few moments. She had many things on her mind. But then she found herself saying, "I want to stay."

Korrev couldn't hide his surprise. "You want to stay with me?"

"And Alice," she couldn't help but say. Karin wasn't a naturally shy person, but saying out loud she wanted to stay with Korrev suddenly made her feel nervous. She had spent so much time trying to get away from him. Then, suddenly, she wanted him near her. It was foolish. Sometimes she couldn't believe her own mind.

Karin should run away. The logical part of her brain told her to accept his offer, but her heart, her heart wanted something different, and it was to stay with him. Forever. Even if it was as his pet or as his breeding mare, she wanted to stay with him. Being torn apart away from him, even if her memories were erased, would be too much for her.

"Are you sure?" Korrev pressed his thumb against her chin, tilting her towards him. "Because once you say yes, there is no going back. I won't let you leave my sight again, Karin. Do you understand?"

"I do," Karin responded. She was surprised her voice wasn't shaking.

A twitch of a smile appeared on his lips and his body relaxed. "Good."

That was all he said. They would probably never say the words "I love you" to each other. Korrev wasn't the type to say them. Neither was Karin.

That was fine. They didn't need to say anything.

Korrev knew what Karin felt about him. Karin knew what Korrev felt about her.

It didn't need to be said out loud. They just knew.

"May I have a kiss?" he asked, sounding so polite, it almost made Karin laugh. He was such a brute and aggressive man, it was hard to imagine him as anything else.

"I should probably have a bath first," she mused. She felt sticky, and not in a good way.

Korrev nodded. "And then?"

Karin giggled. "And then we can kiss."

Fourteen

After one more week of bedrest, Korrev and Azis had finally allowed her to have visitors. Karin guessed Korrev was probably sick of her whining so he just gave in to her whim. Or maybe he felt a bit sorry for her because her cough had returned with a vengeance. Sometimes she would cough so hard, her body would hurt for hours afterwards.

Azis had warned her it might take months for her body to recover from the bouts of poison, but she was doing splendid so far. When she had been told she was lucky to be alive, she had felt quite dumb that she ate the berries in the first place.

Her journey to recovery would be long, but she was hopeful that someday her body would stop hurting as much. Korrev had even taken her on daily walks, even though he fussed over her constantly as if she were as weak as a newborn.

Whatever the reason was for Korrev's rare generosity, she decided to milk it as much as she could. The very first thing she wanted to do was, of course, have Alice visit her.

Karin was in bed—in Korrev's large, fancy canopy bed if she had to be specific. Not in her pet bed. She had finally left the infirmary after pleading with Korrev. She was going to milk the poor-little-me act as much as she could. Korrev was almost spoiling her with attention and giving in to her every whim, something which he hadn't done before. She was going to take advantage of it for as long as possible. She was still weak, and there was no way Korrev would punish her in her condition.

The blonde had asked him for visitors. He had hesitated but agreed to let Alice visit for only one hour. It wasn't much, but she would take whatever she could get.

Alice had changed so much, she hardly recognized her. She was heavily pregnant and round. Practically bursting. But she looked downright adorable with her large belly, even though Alice complained her back and chest ached a lot.

Alice was due soon, which had made Kyvan annoyingly protective. She was surprised he had even allowed her to come, but when the king gave an order, not even Kyvan could say no. Korrev was breaking many rules for her, which made her secretly pleased.

"How are you feeling?" Alice asked warmly as she placed a hand on her large belly.

Karin felt a twinge of jealousy, even though it was stupid to feel jealous of her only friend. She had never wanted children. She had convinced herself she was not going to be a very good mother because her own mother had been shitty. She had made her peace that she was never going to experience pregnancy or carry her newborn in her arms. But seeing Alice looking so heavily pregnant, triggered something in her. Something which she couldn't explain.

Karin wished she could be the one experiencing pregnancy. She wished she would soon be the one giving birth to Korrev's child. She wanted to hold her own baby in her arms. Even though she was a bit disappointed she would only be able to bear male children.

Azis had warned her being bred could not happen for several

months, until her body recovered, which, to be quite honest, just caused her to become more frustrated.

When she had first come to Krotev, Azis had told her she had been given a fertility treatment, but she had been here for more than a year and she had not become pregnant. Alice had been here less time and she would soon have a bouncing baby boy.

She chewed on her cheek nervously. What if she couldn't get pregnant? What if she was infertile? What if she could never give Korrev a baby? Would he dump her? Would he get another mate who could give him children?

The idea of Korrev impregnating someone else filled her with rage. She didn't want Korrev to have another mate. She certainly didn't want him to get someone else pregnant.

Alice cleared her throat, reminding her that she had asked her a question.

"How do I look?" she asked sarcastically.

Alice gave her a little smile, obviously too polite to say anything.

Karin knew she looked horrible. She was struggling to gain weight, she was pale, there were dark circles under her eyes, and her cough made it seem like she had gotten infected by the plague.

"You look perfect. Just like you."

Karin rolled her eyes as she took a sip of water. "You're just like Korrev. A terrible liar. Both of you are too blunt to be dishonest. I know I look horrible."

She had been self-conscious about her appearance when she was a young woman, but Karin would do anything to look like she was once. She looked absolutely ghoulish. What if Korrev lost interest? The idea seemed silly to her, especially since he had done so much to make sure she was rescued.

"It will be over soon," Alice said brightly, like the good-natured person she was. "And then we can resume our playdates. Except now, with a baby in tow."

Karin smiled. That would be nice. Babies were cute, and both Kyvan and Alice were attractive. She was sure their son would be a cutie pie.

A wave of dizziness hit her as she lay back down. "I don't think I'll ever get better. It's been two months since I was rescued and I still feel so tired. All I want to do is sleep and I can barely digest a meal."

"Do the healers know what it is?"

"They said the poison is out of my system, my body is just recuperating, but since I'm human, it takes longer. They're giving me all these tonics and pills, but to be honest, I don't think they're doing much."

Korrev had been forcing her to go visit Azis twice a day, until both Karin and Azis were growing tired of each other.

"I miss the sun," Karin blurted out, breaking the silence. "And the beach. And hot dogs. I regret not going to the beach more when I was in New York. I think I just assumed it would always be there."

Krotev wasn't chilly, but it definitely didn't get as hot here as it did on Earth. The palace was warm since she didn't usually wear clothes, but she hadn't explored Krotev as much as she would like. Not to mention, she was still shy when it came to her nudity.

Alice closed her eyes. "And ice cream and a bonfire with chocolate and s'mores."

"Chocolate. I would give my left arm if I could have a chocolate bar." Karin felt like she could eat three boxes of chocolates. It was the only thing she was truly craving.

"I'm sure Korrev would be more than happy to send for one if it meant you would eat."

Silence.

Korrev might be spoiling her now, but she wasn't foolish enough to expect he would do it forever. For goodness' sake,

Karin didn't even know if she was going to be punished for the stunt she'd pulled. She clenched her buttocks, just thinking about it.

Karin couldn't ask him for chocolate when she didn't even know where she stood with him. She knew he desired her and he didn't want her to depart back to Earth. But what else? Alien men were just as complicated as human men. Why did they have to make everything so complicated?

"Leave him out of this," she murmured as she looked at Alice's pregnant belly again. She wanted to touch it, to feel the baby kick, but she felt too shy to ask her. She had never touched a woman's pregnant belly before. Babies had been the furthest thing from her mind, but now that they might be in her near future, it was all she could think about. "Are you sure you're not pregnant with twins? No offense, but you look like an overindulged cat."

Alice gave her a reproachful look. "Thanks for the compliment. That doesn't terrify me at all."

Karin winced. "Sorry. I've never given birth. I'm sure everything will be fine."

She wasn't even sure how giving birth here worked. Did they have epidurals? She couldn't imagine pushing out such a big baby with no pain medication.

"Have you thought about names?"

"Not really, Kyvan wants to name him after his father, but it's quite a mouthful. I don't think I want to give such a difficult name to a baby. Since I knew it was going to be a boy, I thought it was going to be easier, but no such luck. Do you think you would ever want to have a baby?"

Karin shrugged. "Mates have babies. Pets don't."

"But you don't know if you're a pet anymore."

"Bad pets who run away don't get rewarded. That's what the king said," Karin said flatly. She tried to hide the hurt in her voice, but she was unsuccessful. Yes, he wanted her to stay, but did he want Karin to be the mother of his children? What if he wanted someone prettier or younger? "He will never raise my status to anything but a pet. Why do you think I tried running away? Do you really think he would let a little troublemaker like me give birth to his princes?"

Alice raised an eyebrow. "The question is do you want to give birth to his princes?"

Before she could respond that yes, she wanted to give birth to his babies, Korrev stormed in. He had an impatient look on his face and he was glaring at Alice. He had never liked her and she never understood why. Perhaps, because like Kyvan, she was the only one who didn't seem afraid of him.

"Alice, leave. Now."

He didn't bother to wait until she did to kneel down next to her bed. Korrev squeezed her hand, showing a rare moment of affection in public. "How are you feeling?"

"Much better, my king. Thank you." She looked in Alice's direction, trying to soften his feeling towards her. "Visiting with Alice did me good. You should come back soon and bring your baby with you. I would love to meet him."

Alice glared at Korrev. "You'd better treat her with respect or I will—"

"Of course, I have nothing but respect for my queen." There was a slight smirk on Korrev's lips, indicating he enjoyed the mystified looks on both their faces. Apparently, it had been his goal all along.

Meanwhile, Karin couldn't believe what she was hearing. Queen? Did he want her to be his queen? This was the first time he had addressed her as something else other than Pet.

She stared at him with a mixture of disbelief on her face. "Your queen?"

He pecked her lips. It was like he could have read her mind

and had taken care of all of her insecurities. "Yes, my queen. Once you are well, we will work on siring princes. How does that sound?"

Karin looked completely lost, her mouth opened and closed, but nothing came out. He was going to make her his queen. Never in the history of Krotev, had there been a queen. The king's partner was simply referred to as "mate".

Karin Johansson would be the first queen of Krotev. It was unbelievable.

Korrev's smirk was growing wider by the second while her entire face turned red. She suddenly felt very foolish.

"Good." He turned back to Alice, looking annoyed she was still there. Alice was still in shock at what he had said and hadn't moved. "I believe I dismissed you."

"Yes, of course."

Once they were alone, Karin hoped the words would come to her about what she wanted to say. But she felt just as awkward as ever. What if Korrev had just said he would make her queen to get under Alice's skin?

He began rubbing the back of her hand in circular motions like he always did. She hadn't realized until then, but he often did this when he wanted to soothe her.

"Were you serious about what you said?"

"About what part?"

She threw him a dark look.

"Do you really think so little of me, Pet?"

"Perhaps you were joking. Maybe you didn't mean it."

"When have I ever joked?"

That part was true at least. He never joked.

Korrev shook his head, looking almost disappointed. "I thought you would be pleased. I thought women liked the idea of being queen and wearing a pretty crown on their head."

"I am pleased, but this is so unexpected." Her voice grew

unhappy. "What if your men are not happy I've gone from pet to queen?"

"My men will accept whatever I order them to. The question remains, Karin, do you accept the position as queen?"

Karin squeezed his hand. "I do."

Fifteen

"Please."

"No."

"Please."

Pause.

"No."

"Pretty please?"

"I already said no. Have you become deaf?"

Karin flinched.

For the past few weeks, Korrev had been incredibly gentle. She had gotten used to gentle words, not his sharpness.

Korrev sighed, which was his version of an apology. It had been a few weeks since her visit with Alice, and Karin was barely getting out of bed. Karin had heard, though, that Alice had a bouncing baby boy who weighed eleven pounds at birth. Poor Alice.

She still felt a bit tired, but the nasty tonics she had been forced to consume had done their job. Now, she was heading to Azis to have one final appointment.

"Sorry," she responded meekly. Karin knew Korrev had had a difficult few weeks and she shouldn't push. He had a lot of work to catch up on because he had missed so much trying to catch Karin.

He still hadn't said much regarding a punishment for running away and Karin hoped it remained that way. She hadn't been punished in weeks and she liked sitting down on a rear which wasn't stinging.

"Karin, I do not mean to be short-tempered, but you have been asking me the same question for weeks, and the answer is still no." Korrev sighed. "I will not fuck you until Azis tells me you are well enough for me to breed you again."

Karin tried not to sulk like a little girl. For months, Korrev had been constantly touching her. The one thing she wanted him to do, he actually refused. A week ago, her sexual appetite had come back after she had been bedridden.

After months of not having sex, it was the only thing she could think of. She wanted him. Badly. She wanted him to fuck her as he used to. Long. Hard. For hours on end, until she felt like she was out of breath and her lower body was sore and achy.

If she got pregnant, then it would certainly be a bonus. Korrev had told Kyvan that Alice had made his queen eager for a baby, which had made Kyvan roar with laughter.

Karin wanted Korrev to act like he had in the past. Possessive. Dominating. Instead of treating her gently like he currently was. Who knew the brash king had the ability to be gentle?

She touched her neck. The pink bow collar had not been brought back, but it had been replaced by something else. A diamond and pearl choker now adorned her neck. The choker was beautiful and made of the finest gold, which Korrev said could only be found on one planet. The diamonds and pearls had been brought from Earth so she could have a little piece of home with her.

Korrev had explained that even though he wouldn't go back to the bow collar, he still wanted something he could use to track her down if it was ever needed. Karin thought it was silly, but if it gave him peace of mind, she was fine with it.

Sometimes Karin thought she was in a dream and Korrev would tell her he was joking and she would no longer be queen. But so far, he had kept his promise. He told her they would hold an official ceremony when the weather got warmer and she would be recognized as the first queen of Krotev.

She wondered what a queen did. Probably some sort of charity project, even though Korrev didn't seem like the charitable type.

"Don't pout," Korrev scolded her as he opened the door of the infirmary. "Serves you right. After all, I didn't lie with anyone else while I was searching for you. It serves you well for you to go through the same pain I went through."

Karin scowled. She was tempted to tell Korrev she'd give up her queenship if it meant Korrev would just fuck her.

Azis greeted them with a slight bow. He didn't seem surprised they were here. It seemed Korrev dragged her here twice a day, to convince himself she wasn't dying.

Karin had told him teasingly at the last appointment that she was going to be queen. Azis, being Azis, had not responded, but she had a feeling he disapproved.

Azis was not a man who liked change. Not to mention, he was probably worried he would have to deal with both Karin and Korrev daily.

He led Karin to the back of the room where he usually provided his services.

Korrev stiffened behind them, even though it was clear he wanted to follow them. "I'll be waiting outside."

After her third appointment with Azis, both of them had kicked Korrev out. He had a bad habit of being persistent and overly critical, to the point it drove all of them crazy. Azis never said it, but she knew he was grateful to her for sticking up for him.

"How are you feeling, Your Majesty?" he asked dourly as he started listening to her chest.

Karin let out a small laugh which quite quickly grew into a cough. Azis glared at her. "I am well. You do realize you don't have to address me as 'Your Majesty', right? The coronation is still months away."

Azis pursed his lips. "It is a matter of respect."

She didn't say anything, nor did she bother correcting him. Azis was Azis. If she had learned anything in the past few months since staying in Krotev, it was Azis and Korrev were both stubborn to a fault and it was impossible to change their minds.

Azis went through the rest of the checkup quietly. Afterwards, he gave her what she felt was his own version of a smile. "Everything looks much better than I expected. You should still take it easy for the next few weeks, but you can return to your daily life."

Karin laughed. "Return to the life as a pet?"

"No, madam. To prepare yourself for your new life as queen. The king's family has been ruling Krotev for centuries. Since my own father was a boy. Now, it will be your turn to raise the future princes, the eldest who will, of course, be king."

She winced. Talk about pressure. But she had noticed people were starting to treat her with more respect, even though no official announcement had been made.

Karin fumbled with her fingers since, sick or not, she was still not allowed to wear clothes. "Azis, I did have some concerns."

"About what, madam?"

"I've been in Krotev for a year now. When I first came here, I was injected with a fertility shot. With the exception of the months I was gone, Korrev has been trying to breed me constantly. However, I had never become pregnant once, compared to Alice and the other mates who got pregnant in a matter of months." Her voice broke and she hadn't realized how sensitive she had become until that moment. Nor how much she wanted a baby.

Karin wiped away a loose tear. The last thing she needed was for Azis to see her cry. "I'm just worried I won't be able to become pregnant and I won't be able to give Korrev a son and heir."

Azis looked at her in a way which was almost sympathetic. "You are older than Alice and the majority of the other mates, but it does not indicate you will never conceive. Some younger women have trouble becoming pregnant as well. I can give you another dose of our fertility injection if you are concerned."

Karin nodded as she leaned on her side so he could inject her in her bottom. After spending so much time together, she had become comfortable in her nakedness.

After he had given her the painful injection, she turned to Azis. "How long will it take me to get pregnant?"

"For some, it could take days. Others, weeks. Sometimes months. We just have to be patient."

"What if it takes longer than that?" Karin's voice broke. "I already wasted a year. Korrev wants heirs soon. What if he does not want to wait as long? What if he chooses someone else to carry his babies instead?"

In a rare moment of affection, Azis squeezed her hand. "Korrev will understand. He had waited this long to have a family. He can wait a bit more." He paused. "It took my mother fourteen years to become pregnant with me. I was her only offspring. My father was able to wait. Korrev will wait as well."

Karin smiled, even though she was a bit teary-eyed. "She gave birth to one of the greatest healers in Krotev." She couldn't say for sure, but she thought Azis blushed.

He cleared his throat. "I will run a checkup in six months. If you are still not pregnant, then I will run some tests. Stress can make pregnancy hard to obtain. I advise you to relax your body."

"Is Korrev allowed to breed me?"

Karin wanted to return to their lovemaking soon. Not just because she was horny, but because she wanted a baby soon. It would be nice if her and Alice's sons would be able to grow together, just like Kyvan and Korrev.

He sighed. "Within reason. You should not tire your body out. But yes, you can resume your activities."

Karin gave him a kiss on the cheek which he quickly wiped away. She went outside where Korrev was waiting for her. He raised an eyebrow. "Well?"

Karin wrapped her arms around him gleefully. "You can breed me again!"

He laughed. "That was not my main concern, Karin. Is everything else all right?" Korrev didn't complain, but she knew her sickness had taken a toll on him and he hadn't been acting like a king should.

She gave a quick nod and he kissed the tip of her nose. Karin used the opportunity to rub her body against him.

"Karin!" he snarled at her as he spanked her left butt cheek, leaving behind a bright pink handprint. Her body shivered with glee. "Not in public. I do not want anyone else to see me breed you."

"Then take me back to our room," she purred seductively.

Korrev hesitated, but only for a second. She could see the imprint of his cock in his trousers. He wanted this as much as she did. He just needed a little pushing.

"Please." She lowered her hand and touched him gently. He let out a small hiss when her hand squeezed his manhood.

Korrev scooped her up in his arms and practically dragged her to their bedroom. A small giggle escaped from her lips as she wrapped her arms around his neck.

Korrev closed the door behind himself and plopped her down on the bed. This was one of the good things about always being naked. They were always ready when it was time for their lovemaking.

Karin couldn't remember the last time she felt hornier, and it was almost embarrassing. She looked at Korrev with so much lust in her eyes, she was practically dripping it.

Her blue eyes looked at the way he slowly took off his clothes and the way his cock bounced out of his trousers. He raised an eyebrow. "Karin, I command you tell me if you are ever in pain at any point. Is it understood?"

She nodded impatiently as she patted the opposite side of the bed.

Karin lost count of how many hours they spent making love. It could have been four or six or eight. It didn't matter. All she could think about was the way their bodies were pressed against each other. How Korrev would grip her hips as he thrust in and out of her. How she would caress his muscles while thinking their children would be a carbon copy of both of them. Blonde and blue-eyed.

Karin couldn't remember the last time she had been happier. She hoped she remained that way.

Sixteen

"Your baby is fat."

Kyvan threw Korrev a dirty look as he grabbed his newborn son, Kovin, away from him. Kovin was a chubby baby, with a wide, toothless grin and dark hair and blue eyes like his mother, Alice.

He was two months old, and Korrev already knew he was going to be a fine warrior if the way he was gripping a plushy his mother had lovingly knitted for him was any indication. Alice was having a playdate with Karin, so it was decided both men would take care of Kovin.

Kovin was chewing on his father's bicep, leaving drool all over the place.

At one point, it would have disgusted Korrev, but strangely, he now found it adorable. He now found many things adorable, it seemed.

Kyvan sighed as he touched the back of his son's head. "We have about twenty minutes before he starts throwing a fit and starts screaming for Alice. It seems he's hungry every thirty minutes, which doesn't help me with Alice when I tell her I want another baby soon. The last time I suggested it, she threw a vase at my head."

"But everything else is good?" Korrev asked. Kovin gripped his tiny hand around Korrev's finger and squeezed. He giggled.

"Yes, Azis says the baby is healthy. Alice says the birth wasn't too bad. Perhaps, I'll convince her to have another baby before the year is over."

Korrev laughed darkly. "You do know you don't have to ask much, right? She is your mate. It is her job to give you sons."

"She is also my wife," Kyvan said defensively. Kyvan and Alice had a ridiculous wedding ceremony a month ago, after Alice had insisted on the stupid human ritual. Korrev had only attended because it would have been frowned upon if, as king, he didn't go. He hoped the others didn't get those same ridiculous ideas or he would lose it.

One wedding was bad enough. He was happy Karin was happy with being queen and she didn't need to get married to be happy.

Kovin started fussing with his arms and whining. Korrev sighed as he opened his arms. "Give him to me." Kyvan did as he was told and the king started bouncing the baby on his lap. Kovin laughed and for a few minutes, at least, he stopped thinking about being hungry.

"Is there anything on your mind?" Kyvan asked casually, knowing he wouldn't speak if pressured. "You asked for this play-date out of the blue."

"It's Karin."

"It's always about Karin. She's the only one who manages to change your moods so quickly. What about Karin?"

"You must not tell Alice about this."

"I tell Alice everything. Unless it is a safety matter."

"This is a secret you will keep from her. As your king, I order it."

Kyvan sighed, thoroughly annoyed. "All right, if you insist, but I must warn you there is a high chance Karin is telling Alice about the very matter you are determined to keep so hidden."

Korrev scowled but didn't correct him. Kovin started tugging on his blond hair.

"She can't get pregnant."

Karin had thought this month she had gotten pregnant, but when she went to get checked by Azis, he'd told her there was no baby in her womb.

This had caused Karin to fall into a deep depression, which was why he had insisted to Kyvan for them to have a playdate while the men kept the baby behind. He was worried his queen would grow even sadder if she saw the baby.

Kyvan struggled to hide his surprise. Korrev couldn't blame him. A mate who couldn't get pregnant, wasn't unheard of, but it was rare. They had the best medicine and technology, even better than the human ones and most planets. Azis usually pumped them full of fertility drugs when they first arrived, causing them to become pregnant shortly after they arrived at Krotev.

Korrev had been taming Karin when she had first arrived and then she had run away, so he hadn't thought much about her fertility until Karin had brought it up.

He knew she had gotten another dose of fertility drugs from Azis and he fucked her at least twice a day, but there was still no baby.

Karin was growing desperate, and he quite frankly didn't know how to help her. They had run into this problem with some of his other warriors' mates before. It was rare, but it happened. Sometimes his warriors decided to send their mates back to Earth if they couldn't provide them with children; other times, the couple agreed to remain childless.

They had already established Karin was staying in Krotev, but they had never discussed the possibility she might not have children since it was so rare.

For the first time, Korrev was feeling a bit lost. He didn't want to hurt Karin by getting another mate who could birth him children, but he also couldn't die without providing an heir. There would be chaos.

Kyvan paused, unsure of what to say. "What does Azis say? He's the expert."

He snorted. "He's useless. He says her illness must have caused problems and we should be patient. But she's been here for over a year and she hasn't gotten pregnant. Not even once."

"A year is not very long in our lifespan," Kyvan tried to argue. "Sometimes it takes mates a little longer to be impregnated. I wouldn't lose hope just yet."

"Karin really wants a baby, for different reasons than I do. She's been feeling unnaturally sad." Korrev hesitated. Kyvan's own mother had been killed by his father when she had fallen into a deep depression after his birth. It had been meant as an act of kindness. Kyvan never spoke of it, though. "I am just worried her sadness will continue if she fails to become pregnant."

He nodded. "What will you do then?"

"I need an heir."

"So, will you push her aside?"

It wasn't unusual for a king to have more than one mate.

"No, I want her to be by my side, to be my only queen. Karin would never allow another woman to share my bed." Korrev was proud his queen was so possessive of him.

"But you need an heir," was all Kyvan said. Korrev would need to make a decision soon.

"I know, but I will not hurt Karin. Not again."

Kyvan seemed surprised at his statement. The bastard didn't even try to hide it. The king pursed his lips as the baby drooled all over him.

Korrev pushed the baby towards him. "I think your son needs you."

~

"I wanted to see the baby," Karin whined when he picked her up from her playdate with Alice. The baby had grown fussy with Korrev and Kyvan. Kyvan had decided to take him back to his quarters after the king told him he would drop Alice off.

Alice was only too happy to return to her baby and husband.

Korrev didn't like the look on Karin's face when she saw Alice holding the baby, even though it wasn't Alice's fault. He had just taken Karin back to their bedroom, even though both Alice and Kyvan had invited them to stay for the evening meal.

"You didn't miss much," Korrev insisted gently. "He just cries and wants his mother a lot."

"He's adorable. He gets bigger every time I see him." A sad look crossed her eyes.

He squeezed her shoulder. He was trying to be sympathetic. Korrev truly was, but it didn't come easy to him. Who had ever heard of a sympathetic king? Still, for her, he could at least try.

"You'll get pregnant soon, love. I'm sure of it."

Karin was trying too hard to smile, to please him, but she was struggling to hold it. "I know."

Korrev nuzzled his nose against the back of her ear. "We could have dinner and then go to bed early." He squeezed one of her breasts.

Karin kissed him gently on the lips. "I'm actually going to bed without dinner. I'm not very hungry."

"Karin," he scolded gently. "You will get pregnant soon. I guarantee it."

Karin didn't think it was true, but she didn't seem to be in the mood to argue. Instead, she squeezed his hand in a weak attempt to make him feel better. "I know I will."

The next few days passed, and neither Korrev nor Karin brought up the idea of a baby again. It was still weighing heavily on her mind, he could tell by the miserable look on her face.

She was quiet. He didn't like seeing her quiet because it usually meant she was going to do something crazy without thinking.

Korrev had asked Azis for advice, but of course, he was no help. He had just told him he needed to let nature take its course and to wait a few more months before trying more severe methods.

But he didn't want to wait any longer. Korrev wanted to try something now. Anything to make her happy. He hated seeing Karin so unhappy. Having her pout because of a spanking was one thing, but having her be utterly miserable was something quite different. Karin was getting sadder and sadder each day. She was also losing weight.

He could tell every night when he fucked her. She was losing her curves and becoming skin and bones, which worried him constantly. She had never quite recuperated from her illness and he didn't want her to regress.

"You could take her on a trip," Kyvan suggested one day during one of their training sessions.

"A trip? What kind of trip?" Korrev wiped the sweat off his brow. He was king. He couldn't just go gallivanting across other planets. It could become a matter of national security.

"To Earth." Kyvan gave a small shrug, as if it should have been obvious. "Before her mind was all about babies, she was homesick. Perhaps taking her back to Earth would give her something else to think about."

It wasn't a bad idea, but it did make him worry. What if she suddenly decided she preferred Earth to Krotcv and she changed her mind? Not that he would ever let her leave, of course, but he didn't want to give her another reason to be desperately unhappy.

"Do you think it's a good idea?"

Kyvan gave him a crooked smile. "It's the only option you have, I'm afraid. If Alice and I didn't have the baby to take care of, we would go with you. Unlike you, I actually like Earth." Unlike Korrev, Kyvan had spent a few weeks stalking Alice before he kidnapped her.

"Earth it is." But despite him saying the words, he couldn't hide his doubtfulness.

Karin reacted pleasantly when he told her they would visit Earth. For a few minutes, she stared at him curiously, but at least her mind wasn't on a baby anymore. "You're not planning on dumping me there and getting a more fertile mate, are you?"

Korrev let out a laugh until he realized his future queen was quite serious. "Honestly, Karin, look how much I have suffered for you. Do you really think after everything I've gone through, I would just dump you on Earth?"

Karin rolled her eyes, but an amused smile was twitching on her lips.

"We can't go back to New York," he warned her. "It would be a huge security risk if someone were to recognize you. But we can go anywhere else. Avoiding the entire United States might be the safe option."

She rolled her eyes at his paranoia, but after a few minutes, she finally told him where she wanted to go. "Paris."

The following day, they left on one of the smaller ships, to Paris, France. They would have to land in the French countryside to appear undetected and then board a train or bus. Karin didn't care. She was too excited. For once, she was thinking of something not related to pregnancy.

Karin glanced curiously at the way Korrev navigated the ship. No wonder she had failed so miserably on her first try.

They spent a week in Paris, doing all the touristy things Karin had always wanted to do, but never had because she had put work first. They visited the shops, which Korrev found pointless because she would always be naked at home. They went to museums, which Korrev found boring. They tried delicious French cuisine, which Korrev found tasteless.

At night, Korrev would fuck her so hard, she was surprised they never got a noise complaint. The bed would shake and her moans would only be half hidden by a pillow as he pumped into her, filling her with each stroke. Karin felt like she was still filled with cum even after she had cleaned herself.

On their last day in Paris, Karin had insisted on a walk near the Eiffel Tower. It was August on Earth and very warm, even at night, which hadn't helped Korrev's sullen mood. Laughingly, Korrev hated the heat. He said he had never gotten used to it since Krotev was significantly colder, with the exception of the palace.

It was fun seeing him sweat and dealing with tourists who didn't see him as the almighty alien king.

"Do you miss it?" Korrev suddenly asked as he wrapped his arms around her torso, breathing in her sweet scent.

"Sometimes," she admitted as she looked at a couple walking their dog. "I'd forgotten how busy everything was all the time. How many people there are on Earth. Even though I've lived here for over three decades, it feels surreal. It's like I never left."

"But?" Korrev nibbled on her ear. "I can feel a "but" coming."

Karin let out a small laugh. "I don't want to say it. Otherwise, you are going to get an even bigger head than the one you already have."

"Say it."

"I miss home," she finally blurted out. Karin looked like she couldn't believe she had said it.

A proud smile appeared on Korrev's face even though he tried to hide it.

Karin gave him a whack on the shoulder. "Don't be smug. It's not attractive."

"I'm not being smug. It just pleases me you think of Krotev as home after despising it for so long."

"I didn't despise Krotev, I despised you, for pulling me around on a leash," she answered back snarkily. "But I do miss it, and Alice, of course. Our bed is much more comfortable there. Krotev is so much more peaceful than Earth. I never knew how peaceful until I returned to Earth."

"Do you want to go back?" he asked hopefully. They still had a week left in their travel plans. She had gotten it into her head she wanted to go visit Italy.

Karin smirked. "Nice try. You promised me Italy, and we are going to Italy." She squeezed his hand. "We are going to have the rest of our lives in Krotev. Let's enjoy this moment together, just the two of us."

Seventeen

"Karin, you have to let me go." Korrev tried to unhook Karin's arms which were wrapped around him. Karin's bare breasts were rubbing against his torso and his cock was hard. But he didn't have time for morning sex.

He was behind on meetings because of the time he had spent in Europe. Korrev could not spend more time in bed with his queen, no matter how much he wanted to.

Karin pouted but eventually let him go. "Will you be back for lunch?"

"No." Korrev kissed her forehead as he put on his clothes. "But I will be back for dinner. Make sure you take your nap."

"I will." Karin sulked. "Can I visit Alice and the baby?"

Korrev hesitated.

Karin rolled her eyes. "They live in the palace." She pointed to her choker. "Not to mention, you have this to keep me in line."

"Fine. You can go after you take your nap and before dinner. I don't want to have to chase you down, Karin."

Karin rolled her eyes. Korrev gave her a playful slap on the bottom, causing her to giggle.

After eating lunch and taking a very short nap, Karin made her way to Alice's quarters. Kyvan was not there, so Alice answered the door. Unlike Karin, she was half dressed with the exception of her breasts.

Alice complained she was always constantly leaking or the baby was always hungry. There was no point, she said, in covering up.

Kovin was happily sucking on her breast while poor Alice looked on the verge of exhaustion.

"Are you sure this is what you want?" she asked teasingly as Karin prepared drinks and snacks.

"More than anything." Karin squeezed Kovin's little foot. "Though, hopefully, my babies are only half the size of yours."

Alice let out a small laugh. "I doubt it. Krotev men are large, so it means large babies, unfortunately. Azis has the best medication, though. You won't even feel a thing. Believe me, the pain comes afterwards when the baby is hungry every five seconds and both your son and your mate want your attention at the same time." Alice let out a small laugh. "I was surprised when I found out my son and Kyvan could argue with each other, even though one of them can't talk."

Karin smiled, but she couldn't ignore the pang of sadness she felt in her chest. When she had been in Europe, becoming pregnant had been the furthest thing from her mind, but now she was in Krotev, and it was the only thing she could think about.

Alice sensed she must have said something insensitive because she quickly changed the topic. "How was Europe? Don't leave one thing out. I want to hear all about Korrev riding public transportation and dealing with tourists."

Karin laughed as she told her about the places they visited, the food, and Korrev's lousy mood. She had brought a few gifts back for them. For Kyvan, she had brought a case of French cigarettes, for Alice, some lovely hair accessories, and for Kovin, many little toys he could play with since he was too big to fit into normal baby-sized clothing.

"Thank you, Karin, you have been very generous," Alice replied warmly. "Not to mention, you have managed to distract me from breastfeeding which I greatly appreciate."

"I should get going." Karin kissed her cheek regretfully. "Otherwise, Korrev will throw a fit."

Karin stood up, but suddenly, her knees jerked and her legs felt wobbly. She had to hold on to the edge of the chair to prevent herself from falling.

Alice tore the baby from her chest, leading to a crying fit. "What's wrong? Are you hurt?" Alice tried to soothe her screaming baby while checking on her friend.

Karin shook her head, but she was still feeling a bit dizzy. She bit her lip as she waited for her vision to clear. "No, I just felt dizzy. Like I used to feel after I woke up from eating the berries."

Alice looked worried. "Maybe you should lie down. Here, you can rest on our bed."

"No, really, it's not necessary. I am perfectly all right." Karin tried to stand up again, but another wave of dizziness hit her. She had to sit back down. Even Kovin stopped crying to look at her with wonder. "Maybe I should rest for a bit."

Alice led her to the master bedroom because her other room had been turned into a nursery for the baby. "I'm sorry for being such a bother." Karin's cheeks flushed. This was so embarrassing. "I'm sure I will be okay after a short nap."

"Take all the time you need, sweetheart." Alice draped a blanket over her as she balanced the baby on her hip.

A wave of exhaustion hit her and before she knew it, Karin closed her eyes and fell into a dreamless slumber. She only woke up when she felt someone shaking her awake. "Karin, Karin, Pet, please wake up." Her eyes opened when she heard Korrev's voice. He still called her "pet" at times, but it was now used as a term of endearment.

When she woke up completely, she saw Alice and Kyvan standing by the doorway. The baby was no longer with Alice, which meant he must be in the nursery. How long had she slept?

"Alice told us you weren't feeling well." Korrev cupped her face in his hand as if checking for a fever. "Was it your stomach?"

"No," she admitted. "It was just a dizzy spell. I'm sure it's nothing." She tried to get out of bed, but another wave of dizziness hit her.

Korrev managed to grip her by her waist, to prevent her from falling. "Karin," he hissed at her, "stay still."

She reluctantly did as she was told.

Korrev scooped her up in his arms as if she were a new bride and took her out of the room without saying anything else to their friends, much to her embarrassment.

"Do you think these are remnants from the berries you ate months ago?" he asked her as he tucked her into bed.

"No, I've been feeling fine. I didn't experience dizzy spells in Europe. I'm sure I'll be fine tomorrow."

But the next day, she was just as sick if not worse. Even getting out of bed to go to the bathroom proved to be a hassle.

Despite her protests, Korrev dragged her to Azis after breakfast, convinced she was dying.

Azis didn't look at all pleased to see either of them as he ran a series of tests which made Karin feel very sore.

When he finished with the examination, he turned to her with what, apparently, was his version of a smile. "Congratulations, my queen. You are pregnant."

For a few minutes, there was nothing but silence. Then Karin let out a loud squeal as she wrapped her arms around Azis. "Are you serious? Am I truly pregnant? Please tell me you're not joking."

He pursed his lips as her king pulled her away, apparently not very happy she was hugging him.

"I am not the joking type, Karin."

"How far along am I?"

"Only a month. But if you're getting dizzy spells so early in the pregnancy, I am concerned it might be very difficult for you. You must rest as much as you can and follow every instruction I give you."

She nodded as she touched her still flat belly. "Oh, I will. I promise I will be very well behaved." Karin turned back to Korrev, who was looking at her with an amused expression on his face. "Oh, Korrev, we are going to be parents."

"Yes, Karin, I did hear him. I also heard the part where you must have plenty of rest." He squeezed her hip. "How many checkups should she have?"

"I would like to check her every week for the first trimester and every month afterwards."

Karin was hardly listening to him. She was acting like an overexcited puppy. "I'm going to have a baby."

Korrev chuckled at her adorableness. "Our first little prince."

"Congratulations on your pregnancy," Alice said, smiling as both women watched her son play with the toys Korrev and Karin brought back from Paris. Kovin was currently busy stuffing the arm of a stuffed bear in his mouth, covering it with saliva.

"Thank you." Karin covered her stomach even though it was still flat. It had only been a few days since Azis had confirmed her pregnancy, but she kept looking at her flat belly as if expecting some sort of miraculous growth.

"I think all you needed was some rest and relaxation. Not to mention a bit of Parisian romance." Alice winked as she stopped Kovin from putting a small block in his mouth. "I'm happy for you, Kar. It will be fun raising our babies together. Plus, we know they will all be boys so they will be best friends."

Karin hesitated. "Please tell me the birthing part is completely painless."

Alice laughed. "Unlike on Earth, Azis prefers to use the strongest medication possible so he doesn't have us screaming in his ear. The healing part afterwards is a bit tedious, but not as much as it would be if we were giving birth on Earth. Why do you think so many mates keep having babies? If it were painful, Krotev's birthing rate would be low. I could come over after the birth for a few days and help you if you want. I'm sure Kyvan can take care of Kovin."

Karin laughed. "Thank you, but I'm sure Korrev wants to do all of the taking care of."

Alice rolled her eyes. "That doesn't surprise me. I'll be surprised if he even lets Azis help you with the birth. He might just do it all himself. Have you thought of a name?"

She shook her head. "No, Krotev names are so strange, but at the same time, human names like John and Andrew wouldn't suit them, either."

"Pick something simple and not too strange." Alice picked up Kovin and hugged him tightly. "That's what I did."

"I look like a fat cow!" Karin whined as she looked at herself in the mirror. She was only six months pregnant, but she looked like she was about to pop. The baby was big and in a breech position, refusing to move. He was apparently as stubborn as his parents.

She had heard Azis and Korrev arguing about a C-section, but she decided she would worry about it when the time came. It wouldn't be her decision in the end, anyway.

She moved her hips slightly, hoping she would look smaller, but she only looked bigger. Karin puffed up her cheeks in frustration. At this point, she didn't want to imagine what she would look like at nine months.

Korrev, who was standing a few feet away from her, raised an eyebrow. "You were the one who wanted to become pregnant so badly. What did you expect? For you to remain slim your entire pregnancy? Females swell up during pregnancy. Everyone knows that."

"I know, but no one wants to hear it." She glared at Korrev. The man was so insensitive at times, she was surprised she had never pummeled him to the ground.

Her breasts, worst of all, had grown so full and heavy that walking, let alone jogging, had become a pain. She had worn a bra for a week or two, but she couldn't stand those, either. It seemed she had gotten used to being nude all the time.

Korrev came forward, wrapping his arms around her as he kissed her. "It will be over soon, you'll see, but for what it's worth, I've never seen you look more beautiful."

~

"It's taking too long." Karin tried to keep her voice from shaking but found out she couldn't. She was too nervous and it seemed Azis had been working on her for hours when, in reality, it was probably only thirty minutes.

"It will be over soon, love," Korrev soothed her as he brushed back a piece of her blonde hair away from her face. "Just relax. Azis and the other healers are working as fast as they can." He glared at them. "Right?"

"I warned you we should have put her to sleep," Azis mumbled from the other end. "But you wouldn't listen."

During the last month of her pregnancy, Karin's feet had swollen and she had grown increasingly tired. Eventually, Azis had suggested, for her and the baby's safety, it was better that they perform a C-section.

Azis had wanted to put her to sleep, but she had refused because she wanted to see the baby. Of course, Korrev had backed her up on it, much to Azis' disappointment.

Korrev squeezed her hand tightly. He wasn't one for many words, but she knew he would be with her and their child always.

She heard a loud cry and felt her shoulders relax. Korrev kissed her quickly on the forehead before he went towards his son and heir.

"Ten pounds and three ounces," Azis announced proudly as he cleaned him up. "Healthy and fit. The future king of Krotev."

"Can I see him?" Karin whined. "I want to see him, Korrev." She was heavily medicated and couldn't get up.

Korrev took the baby from Azis and presented him to her. The baby was still crying angrily. His skin was dark gray, like Korrev's when he was in his alien form, his eyes red. Korrev had said, eventually, the baby would be able to control both his human and alien transformations, but his alien form would become more apparent when he was upset.

"He's so beautiful," she whispered. She was grateful for the distraction while Azis was stitching her up. "Can I hold him?"

"Of course." Korrev settled him in her arms while he kept his hand against the baby's head.

As soon as Karin held him, the gray skin and red eyes started to disappear; replacing them were pale skin which had turned pink from crying, angry blue eyes, and wheat-blond hair. Her son looked at her curiously.

Karin felt her heart was close to bursting by how happy she was feeling. "Hello, sweetheart." She kissed the top of his head. "I'm your mama."

Epilogue

Four years later...

"I'm going to fill you with my seed," Korrev growled in Karin's ear. His queen was lying down on their bed, her pale skin flushed as he pumped into her aggressively, not giving her time to rest. It wasn't like she needed it, though. Even though their lovemaking exhausted her, she was still hungry for more. "And I won't stop until I put another baby in you."

Karin's blue eyes widened as she let out something between a mixture of a groan of protest and a moan. She didn't even try to pull away. She knew Korrev would always get his way and make her his.

Korrev pressed a hand against her swollen lips. "Shh, my queen, you'll wake the little monsters."

Karin and Korrev had been together for more than four years, and in those four years, she had become the first Queen of Krotev as well as giving birth to three healthy half alien, half human princes who were just a few feet away, sleeping in the nursery.

However, the oldest of the three, Pakhen, easily got out of his bed and could drag his brothers along with him even if Karin still saw him as a baby at four years old. Their three sons adored their mother with the same ferocity as their father did.

Karin loved them as well. She would give up her life for her babies, even for her husband. But it did not mean she wanted to get pregnant again.

She had delivered three babies in four years. As soon as Azis would tell her she was healed from the birth, Korrev would practically mount her and fuck her until she became pregnant again.

"No more babies," Karin groaned as Korrev finished inside her. She knew her words didn't mean much. Korrev may love her and she may be queen, but he still had the final say.

When she had first been brought to Krotev, she had been given a painful injection to slow down aging. If they weren't careful, they would end up with a dozen babies. Not that Korrev seemed to mind.

He turned out to be a much better father than Karin thought he was going to be. He was strict but loving and his sons respected him in the same way they adored their mother. Being a father had softened him up, but not so much that he had stopped punishing her altogether.

Karin smiled at the idea. Most "punishments" ended with extremely long lovemaking sessions which Karin didn't seem to mind too much.

"But we make such adorable babies," Korrev cooed as he kissed her.

"Don't try to be cute." She tried to give him a scolding look, but she was failing. "My body is tired, Korrev."

"Fine. I guess we do not have to have a baby this year." He had the audacity to actually look disappointed, even though she had already given birth to three heirs. "Though might I remind you, you were the one who desperately wanted a baby. I am just fulfilling my end of the deal."

"Korrev." Karin gave him a warning look. "Three babies is enough. I'm thirty-seven. I am not exactly a spring chicken anymore." But to be fair, she still looked thirty-three. She had to give it to Krotev aliens, they really were advanced when it came to scientific experiments.

"We'll see," he simply said as he gave her another kiss.

He was a doting father compared to most men, both human and alien. Their children adored him. Sometimes more than their own mother. Neither Karin nor Korrev worried about the future of Krotev.

"I wouldn't say no to a daughter, though," she said slowly. Karin had been thinking about this for a while. Thanks to the Krotev alien genetics, she would only be able to give birth to boys. She had been longing for a little girl. "There are plenty of baby girls who don't have parents. Who won't be missed, I mean." She didn't think Korrev would be too happy if she mentioned getting pregnant with someone else's sperm.

Thankfully, Korrev didn't immediately dismiss the idea. "A princess," he mused, "would be good to form alliances."

That had not been what Karin had in mind.

She rolled her eyes. "I'm sure it would benefit our sons to have a sister as well. This way, they will know how to behave around women when it's time for them to mate, and not act like cavemen." She bit her lip. "I wouldn't want our daughter to be far away from home."

He shrugged. "She could marry Kyvan and Alice's eldest son. Then she would never have to be far away from us."

Kyvan and Alice had four sons and had moved out of the palace two years ago, to a much bigger house on the outskirts of town. Kyvan still worked for Korrev as his right-hand man and Alice and Karin still had playdates, but for their children instead of themselves.

Karin flushed happily. "It would make me very happy."

"Good." Korrev kissed her and he was about to press himself against her again when they heard a baby crying. It was their youngest child, Hekyn, who was only three months old and even more fussy than his two older brothers. He sighed. "Perhaps we should wait until Hekyn stops crying every hour before we get a daughter."

Karin gave him a playful smack as she put on her robe. "He doesn't cry every hour, only when he's hungry. He'll grow out of it eventually, like the others."

Korrev muttered something under his breath which she chose to ignore while she went to console her crying son. She pushed the door of the nursery open. Her two eldest sons, Pakhen and Kov, were thankfully fast asleep. They were four and three years old.

Her three children were a copy of their father, with their golden hair, wide nose, and hot temper. But their blue eyes were the same shade as hers and they had the same small ears.

Karin quickly picked up Hekyn. The last thing she needed was for her older children to wake up, then no one would get any sleep. She started rocking him to sleep before pressing him to her breast after she loosened her robe.

The baby started sucking hungrily, his cries soon diminishing. She squeezed him tightly. She wished they could stay in the baby stage forever. She already knew her sons would be difficult to manage when they became teenagers. Karin could barely handle the baby stage.

"He's asleep; that was fast." Korrev wrapped his arms around her waist.

"I think he needed to be soothed, like another big baby I know," Karin teased him as she put the baby back in the crib.

Korrev scowled as he gave her ass a quick slap.

She giggled.

"Let's go to sleep, Pet. We have a long day tomorrow."

Karin followed her mate. Her king. As she always would.

Annabelle Marin

Annabelle Marin is a twenty-something romantic who lives in sunny California. When she isn't writing she enjoys daydreaming, watching way too much TV, and cuddling with her pets.

Her books are sweet erotic romances with domestic discipline. In her books you can expect: a spoonful of sweetness, a dash of sass, a cup of naughtiness, and an abundance of romance.

You can follow Annabelle on Facebook, Instagram, Goodreads, and Bookbub for exciting updates on upcoming books!

Facebook-https://www.facebook.com/annabelle.marin.940/
Instagram-https://www.instagram.com/missannabellemarin/
Bookbub-//www.bookbub.com/profile/annabelle-marin
Goodreads-www.goodreads.com/author/show/21061973.
Annabelle_Marin

Don't miss these exciting titles by Annabelle Marin and Blushing Books!

Stand Alone Titles

Endless Paradise
Between Kisses & Lies
Letters to Holly
On the Dotted Line
His Southern Belle

12 Naughty Days of Christmas 2021

Blushing Books

Blushing Books is one of the oldest eBook publishers on the web. We've been running websites that publish spanking and BDSM related romance and erotica since 1999, and we have been selling eBooks since 2003. We hope you'll check out our hundreds of offerings at http://www.blushingbooks.com.

Blushing Books Newsletter

Please join the Blushing Books newsletter
to receive updates & special promotional offers.
You can also join by using your mobile phone:
Just text BLUSHING to 22828.